WHISPER OF A KISS

". . . One of the Most Dramatic Love Stories Ever Told"

Stephen W. Hoag, Ph.D.

Inspiring Voices®

Inspiring Voices books may be ordered through booksellers or by contacting:

Inspiring Voices
1663 Liberty Drive
Bloomington, IN 47403
www.inspiringvoices.com
1 (866) 697-5313

ISBN: 978-1-4624-1242-6 (sc)
ISBN: 978-1-4624-1241-9 (hc)
ISBN: 978-1-4624-1243-3 (e)

Library of Congress Control Number: 2018910223

Print information available on the last page.

Inspiring Voices rev. date: 09/18/2018

Contents

Forward

"Whisper of a Kiss" is a dramatic love story that begins as a common narrative of a marginalized young man, Kyle, bestowed with God-given gifts, but as yet unaware of the greatness that sleeps within him. One person, Denise, unintentionally touches his life in some rather profound ways and this young man soars to heights of achievement and personal growth exceeding all expectations.

Since the earliest of times in teaching, learning and schools, some students are seen as shy, quiet, timid or classified as introverts. In current times young people who demonstrate a reserved or reclusive demeanor are viewed as "marginalized". Despite the relative size of the schools or the width of the hallways, these are the students who seem to hug the walls as they move from location to location. Marginalized students are great observers of all that is going on around them, even though they generally feel detached from the energy and emotion that pervades the high school environment.

It is easy for students and faculty to ignore these students as they truly are denizens of the physical margins of the school environment, wishing not to be noticed and usually are not. It is as isolated a school existence as it would seem and just as lonely.

Many factors lead to a child, a student, becoming marginalized. Clearly, the absence of an advocate in the home is a principle contributor. The challenges brought about by the proliferation of single parent domestic settings, and the subsequent economic burdens requiring that a parent hold multiple jobs, while addressing the needs of family members, has, to some degree, limited the services of a parent to each child. We can assume the presence of parental love even in the most trying of family settings, but "time", or better put, the absence of time for parenting for each juvenile in the home, has placed a child to be more than reasonably responsible for their every need, not including the common duty of a child to provide for the care of other children in the home.

History is replete with those who in the early years of life were known to be shy, unassuming and opaque, but who went on to lives of notability. For all with eyes to see, ears to hear and souls of caring, there are far too many young men and women who are not brought forth from obscurity and never empowered to seek the undiscovered talents of their souls.

These wonderful young people are those who often fall through the cracks of their formal education, never uncovering the promise of their lives. Unfortunately, they are often disregarded, left on the margin of a complex school society, never finding that place of belonging.

To understand the "marginalized student" we must first acknowledge that they are observers of all that swirls around them. Keen witnesses of others, they want to experience all the things that others do and often quietly celebrate the moments that other students are experiencing. Unfortunately, the marginalized begin to believe that they are NOT worthy of the basic happiness, range of emotions and high levels of achievement. It is common for them to envy others and consider the "what-if's" of their lives, glorifying and rationalizing the absence of their perceived shortcomings, the most exquisite of which is ... LOVE.

This is a tale of so many young people in today's society who seek to understand the complexities of love and emotion in the ever burgeoning midst of conflicting influences generated by technology, and the absence of a common family language and home environment.

Love is still and always will be the most powerful of emotions, but "Whisper of a Kiss" takes you on an amazing journey, discovering that love is far more than an emotion, "love is an act of will". Love sustains us in times of great challenge while providing moments of resplendent joy. As with all stories founded on the principle of love, it is never a straight path without exposure to the vulnerabilities made possible by love.

The character, Avril is the embodiment of many wonderful single mothers, who love and serve their children with courage. The main character in this narrative, Kyle is far more than a fictitious young man. He is the personification of many hundreds of young men who were, still are, and forever will be students of Stephen W. Hoag, most of which have been part of the Developing Tomorrow's Professionals (DTP) program. As for "The Girl", the woman, the inspiration, DENISE, of this love story, there can be only one.

This book is a celebration of the impact that one person can have on another person's life.

There is Only One

There is an old, time honored adage that "there is someone out there for everyone".

Far beyond that superficial statement that rings full of hope for anyone who takes the time to consider the most important aspects of their lifetimes, is this, "There is **only** one."

Indeed for every man, there is but one girl, THE girl, who ...

... Awakens every sensation that is inherent in the human heart, mind, and body;

... Brings forth a spring of joy with just a momentary thought of her;

... Speaks with a voice that engenders peace, understanding, and patience;

... Raises the senses to heights that no other girl will ever approach;

... Singularly defines beauty from the first glance that will never change regardless of circumstance, or the passage of time.

Countless girls will cross the path of each young man, but only one will take his heart to heights that cannot be replicated. She may never become his friend, lover or wife, but through the miraculous nature of love with its often overwhelming mosaic of sensitivities, a standard of the heart will be established for his lifetime. If the contours of life's circumstances smile kindly on the boy and THE girl, there will never be a limit to their shared love and the experiences such love brings forth.

To be sure, such a love is rare as there is an endless stream of people and daily occurrences that may interrupt the path of two people so wonderfully attuned. The time and timing of life itself will not slow and choices presented to each person are often compromises leading to hope driven selections. We each seek the best outcomes from every relationship, albeit family, friends or co-workers, but we are often left disappointing or wanting.

In the quiet of one's thoughts in those infrequent moments of self-recollection, that one person, THE girl, is there, never altered or reconstituted. She is pristine, perpetually perfect, appearing resplendent until the finality of life.

THERE IS ONLY ONE!

Chapter 1

The First Teacher, a Mother

It is a few days before the onset of the fall of Kyle's junior year of high school; he had already resolved that this would be another tedious nine months of boredom and aloneness in the uncomfortable surroundings of the school building. There would be no attitude of a "fresh start" to the new school year as there was no person that he looked forward to seeing or renewing acquaintances.

Still clearing his eyes from the evening's sleep Kyle walked the ten steps from his bedroom to the kitchen where his mother, Avril was ironing a white uniform for her morning job at a senior citizen facility. Kyle grabbed a breakfast bar from the counter and sat across from his mother who hardly looked up at him as she fastidiously ironed the creases in her uniform.

Avril, just 34 years old, a slightly built woman with a wonderful smile and darting eyes had become something other than what her high school friends might have envisioned. Bubbly and so popular during her early life, she had become reserved and protective of Kyle and their little corner of the world. She like many young women had been forced into her current life style due to circumstances caused by the misjudgments of her youth.

Kyle loved his mother very much and had great admiration for her holding down two jobs so they could have an apartment, a used car and the basic things to live comfortably. Kyle didn't see much of his mother during the week because of her two jobs and missed the talks they used to have in the evening when she was only carrying one job.

As Avril continued to press her clothing to the hssssssing noise of the steam iron, she began a conversation that Kyle had heard many times during these past years, "Kyle you need to become more than a mediocre student this year. Time is running out on your high school years and your grades are just C's and B's.

Kyle rolled his eyes, "Mom, all you do is complain about my grades. I really don't like school and I do enough to get by and I will graduate on time".

Avril raised her eyes to him with a degree of scorn, "Kyle where do you think you can go to college with grades like yours? What do you want to do with your life? It's time to get serious before it's too late"

"Mom, I don't even know if I want to go to college. I hate school. I'm always bored and there is nothing there that interests me, so why go to college".

Avril sensed an argument approaching and having a disagreement with her only son who she had committed her life to was not something worthy to begin her day. She put down her iron and walked around to the other side of the table and placed a kiss on top of his head, something she had done many times over the years.

Reaching into her recent thoughts she opened a topic that she wasn't sure would be received well by her son. "Kyle, you know what I think would be an idea worth considering?"

He immediately perked up thinking that his mother had decided to finally purchase a laptop computer. Kyle was about to discover that his mother had something far different in mind.

"Kyle", she began, "I think you would really benefit from having your own personal mentor."

"MENTOR", he responded, "Why would I need or want a mentor? I don't cause any trouble. I never miss school. A mentor? ... That's a ridiculous idea mom."

Avril looked at her son with caring eyes and began to cry. The notion of a mentor for Kyle was overdue in her judgment, delayed by the continuing sense of guilt she held in her heart.

As she held her face to his head with her arms wrapped around him, she remembered the conversation that she first had with her son when he was just 10 years of age, a talk that resulted in a single question that Avril could not bring herself to answer. Since his earliest days, he would ask, "Mommy, how come I don't have a daddy like the other kids"?

Avril, who always thought and spoke with her heart, suffered each time they both came to the precipice of that important question and the subsequent answer that inevitably was unavoidable. Avril would placate Kyle as best she could with the response, "That's a good question and someday when you are old enough I will explain that to you."

Kyle was confused by his mother's unwillingness to explain why he didn't have a father and figured that it must be something really bad. Maybe his father was dead. Maybe his father was in prison or on a secret mission ... and maybe his father just didn't want anything to do with him. All these conjured up answers to this single question by which Kyle increased his desire to be alone. Often fearful around other children, he dreaded the possibility of being asked about his father. To that end, when Kyle was invited to a birthday party or someone else's home, Kyle would always decline or get emotional if his mother pressed the issue of his attendance.

The answer to that question, although seemingly simple to utter, was in and of itself, the tragic story of a girl's early life ... Avril's life. The answer cut through her heart. It never released its hold on her and there wasn't a day when some manifestation of its reality didn't enter her mind.

A pretty and popular girl in high school, she was her parents' every pride and joy. In their late 40's when Avril was born, they had tried for years to have a child and when Avril came into their lives, it was the answer to every prayer they had ever held sacred. They raised their only daughter, Avril with every privilege, dancing and singing lessons, a fine Catholic private elementary school education. She was an intelligent, charming, beautiful daughter with her parents' high expectations of college matriculation, a career and beyond. Avril and her parents were living the dream.

It all came to an end for them as Avril became pregnant during her junior year in high school and gave birth to Kyle when she was just 17 years old.

Her parents, shocked, dismayed, and unable to regain their balance, were less than supportive in this all too common family dilemma.

Before becoming pregnant she had earned consistent honor roll status and was a member of a number of high school clubs and organizations, earning the plaudits of her high school and community. That all came to an end when she learned she was pregnant. Her parents felt that there was no choice to be made as they assumed the decision-making for Avril to have the baby, requiring her to leave school.

To make matters all the more painful, Avril's high school boyfriend of a year, the father of the baby, claimed that the child was not his and stated that he would shoulder no burden for the child, a position backed by the boy's parents. Wishing to avoid any more scandal, Avril's parents did not pursue legal action, consequently, all responsibility for the baby rested with Avril and her parents.

The world of excitement and opportunity she had known only months before had now shrunk to the size of a postage stamp as her parents made decisions to minimize the impact of the situation and despite their conversations with Avril to the contrary, it seemed their own sense of embarrassment exceeded all other considerations and drove the decisions that were being made.

Avril was to be placed in a school for pregnant girls where she would stay until the baby was born. There were many students Avril included in her circle of friends in high school, but few, if any, would try to contact her while she watched the days pass as a pregnant teenager. It was scary for her and even though the other residents of the school were also pregnant and shared their stories and circumstances, Avril longed for her home and the way of life she knew only a short few months ago.

Avril graduated high school but did so as a single mother. There was help along the way from agencies and her parents, but before long Avril was holding down a job and raising her son ... by HERSELF. The advantages of her early life notwithstanding, Avril was a young woman of incredible character and fortitude. Despite the inherent pressure by her parents to give the child up for adoption, Avril stood tall and courageous before her parents and insisted that this was her son, and she, his mother, would raise him.

Chapter 2

A Time to Talk

It was July 2nd and a day that Avril would always remember. On this day, she could wait no longer. Kyle has to have an answer to his question, "Why don't I have a daddy"?

There were no support systems or family members to call upon for assistance. Both of Avril's parents had died, her father just in the last year. This was one of many times that she handled tough circumstances alone with only her faith in God to see her through, but this one would require extra inner strength and God's help.

It was right around 11:00 am, Saturday and Kyle was sitting at the kitchen table looking at his mother's cellphone. Avril sat down and looked at her son with those loving eyes he had seen many times before. Kyle looked over at his mother and said, "Mom if you don't want me to fool with your phone, I won't".

Avril smiled gently and shook her head and told him that there is something they had to talk about.

With that Avril began, "Kyle you have asked me many times if you have a father. Well, son of mine, the answer is yes you do, but I do not know where he is and I don't' think he wants for us to find or contact him. Both Kyle and Avril began to cry as the young son came over to his mother and hugged her as never before.

Avril soaked in the tears of a dozen *almost* conversations with Kyle explained, "Your father and I were friends in high school, very close friends. I loved him, and you, Kyle, were created out of that love, but your father was not ready to understand what love means. This is the hardest thing to explain to you, what I mean by "love". She continued, "Love is the most beautiful and powerful thing in the world. It makes you feel good in so many ways, but it is also so hard to understand at times."

Kyle's arms were still around his mother's neck as she talked quietly to her young son. Kyle's tears fell upon his mother's face and shoulders and he asked, "Mommy if you loved my father, how come he didn't love you"?

Avril hung on to whatever emotional control she had remaining and sensitively responded, "Kyle, it is so difficult to know how someone else feels about you. Someone can say, "I love you" like I say to you, but it is what they do to show their love. The words matter, but what matters more is what someone does to make you feel loved and wanted, and needed. It is hard to understand, I know, but when you are loved by another person, you can feel it and that feeling becomes part of you.

This talk of "love" confused Kyle and his thoughts and words were cluttered and disjointed trying to understand, especially as it related to his father.

Avril pushed slightly back from their embrace so she could look into her son's face. The tears from both of them covered their faces as Avril's eyes sparkled in appearance and warmth.

Kyle's thoughts began to clear through the emotion of the moment and asked, "Do you think that my father knows who I am and loves me?"

Avril reached deep and just let her heart speak, "I don't know, but all you can do is to be the best Kyle you can be every day and don't worry who loves you, but who you love and how you love them".

Chapter 3

Find your Ways to Love

In an instant, Kyle was filled with questions as any child his age would and, he couldn't get them out of this mouth fast enough.

Kyle looked at his mother and becoming louder and more direct, asked, "Mom, I don't think I understand love too much. It's like you are describing some kind of magic.

"Son, don't worry, sometimes it takes a long long time, many years for adults to figure out what love means", offered the now smiling Avril.

Kyle needed to know more and fought his youthful bewilderment to understand. "Mom you said that ... <u>it is what you do to show love</u> that is more important than saying the words, *I love you*, right?"

"Correct Kyle", Avril answered.

"So, ... Mom, how do you show love?"

Avril, pursed her lips together, ending with a slight smile and looking proudly of her son of usually few words and fewer questions, answered, "Kyle, for each person you love, YOU have to find your own ways to love them. You don't demonstrate love the same way with everyone. Loving someone is giving of the best of yourself to each person in the ways they need. Someday there might be a person in life who needs your love by listening to them. For another, it might be encouraging someone who is feeling sad. Then, someday, there will be an extra special person who needs everything wonderful that is inside of you".

"Mom", Kyle carried on, "like what is wonderful inside me"?

Avril could only shake her head in disbelief at her young son's desire to understand, "Kyle someday, there will be someone who needs to just hear your voice, whether a whisper or a laugh. She will need you to give of yourself in creative loving ways that no one else in the whole world can do but you ...".

Kyle almost in a rude tone, "Mom mom mom, did you say ... "SHE".

Avril could only smile and and nod, "Yes son, there will be a she. You will know a lot of girls in your life.

Kyle bounced back, "Mom, a girl ... and me? Never!"

Now, his mother felt the need for an important teaching moment.

"Son, for everyone of us, ... THERE IS ONLY ONE! One who will hold your heart in her hand and look at you in a way that no one else ever could before. This ONE person will bring all of your best together, ... from your head and all of the thoughts it brings forth, ... your heart and all of the remarkable good feelings gathered up inside of you, ... and in your soul, the spirit of God and those God-given gifts that HE has given you and will never take back."

There is ONLY ONE and she is the only one who can do this. She is out there.

Kyle looked at his mother with confusion, puzzled that this sort of topic is coming up at this time when he feels so alone and isolated from the world around him.

Avril continued, "Kyle, I never found "the one" for me. I thought I had in high school, but he didn't bring all three parts of me together. That's the mistake people make. You can feel great happy emotions with another person, but unless that person brings out the best of your mental capabilities and the fullest realization of your God-given gifts, you haven't found, THE ONE.

Avril hugged her son once again knowing that an incredible event was just shared between them. Much of the guilt she carried for so long seemed to be lifted and she would pray that something special would happen in her son's life because of the day's discussion. Avril had no illusions, she knew that emotions, especially those that are held deep in the recesses of our soul, can creep up on you. They don't go away all that easily.

Before bed Avril took a moment to thank God for the day and to prayerfully ask that Kyle retain the best of their conversation. She prayed, God, let him FIND HIS WAYS TO LOVE.

Chapter 4

Robert, A Mentor

The casual mention of a mentor for Kyle brought back the events of the past and the guilt Avril harbored for not being able to provide a father or male presence in Kyle's life. Her thoughts precipitously flew backwards to her past before there was a Kyle. The routine of the day ... of her life that had all too suddenly become too heavy to carry. Caring for, and about, a child can include a painful mixture of guilt, fear and the second guessing of past decisions.

Avril worked with great diligence to raise Kyle as a polite, respectful person, but the amount of time available to be with him was limited. Early on she placed him in daily child care and although Kyle was well treated and showed continuous growth, Avril lived with pangs of guilt because she wasn't there with Kyle to offer the around the clock care she so wanted to provide.

Once old enough for public school, Avril committed herself to enhance her son's skills in reading and writing. During his elementary school years, he enjoyed the company of fellow students, but with each passing year, it seemed that he was more and more isolated with his own thoughts and distanced himself from much in the way of youthful friendship. By this time, Avril was working in a more demanding job and trying to take courses at a local community college. She had little social life as any free time available was spent with Kyle. In spite of her efforts to give Kyle every bit of the love and time she could offer, Kyle became more disinterested in any type of activities, declining the opportunity to join youth athletic teams, church groups, and school clubs.

By the time he started middle school, Kyle was alone after school most of the time at home as his mother was laid off from her full time job and had to take two part time positions to pay the bills. Kyle found some enjoyment in reading and writing, but unlike most of the kids in school, he did not have a cellphone. There was a landline telephone in the apartment in which they lived, and his mother had a cellphone, although Kyle rarely saw her on it.

As the years passed Avril became more and more protective of Kyle, refrained from dating, not wishing to fall in love, afraid to make a bad decision that could affect Kyle's life.

Kyle's first two years in high school were uneventful with the only notable exception being his near perfect attendance his freshman year, followed by a severe drop-off in lateness and absenteeism his sophomore year. Avril tried to change her work schedule to help him get to school and on time, but her employer was unwilling to help. Avril had grave concerns about his attendance in school as his junior year was about to start.

Avril knew and was sure, that a mentor would make a difference in Kyle's life and now the task at hand was to convince Kyle.

As Avril soft-peddled the idea of Kyle getting a mentor, she called her few friends, her son's school, and the nearby university to find a person who would serve as Kyle's mentor and meet the muster of her requirements. Avril was not sure what the requirements should be for a mentor for her son, but she was positive about what she didn't want.

One day she received a telephone call from the university's school of education. A woman, who identified herself as Jesse, asked if Avril would like to come in and meet with a possible candidate for Kyle's mentor position. Avril did not have much of a positive feeling going into this meeting, but go she did.

Agreeing to meet during her lunch break, Avril would not have much time to size up this college student for the mentorship. Jesse met her at the appointed time and location and ushered her into a small meeting room where this tall handsome college student was seated. He introduced himself as Robert and proceeded to tell Avril about his background. Robert was a graduate student in business, a former athlete at the university and an out-going charmer. There wasn't anything not to like about Robert, except for one thing. He was nothing like her son. Avril thought this might be an oil and water matchup, but right now, Robert was the only game in town.

Robert and Avril began an open discourse, both offering up questions and answers on many topics. Finally convinced that Robert was the right person even before Kyle met him, Avril offered up an insightful outline of what she demanded of this mentorship. "Robert, you are to be a good listener. Kyle must be free to talk. You must encourage him, but never demand that he do something. Please offer advice when Kyle or the moment calls upon you to do so, but your advice must be something he will understand and have staying power. You are not to be his cheerleader or his comfy-cozy friend. Kyle must develop confidence in you and he will, in turn, become confident."

Avril returned to work with the task of getting Kyle to agree to be mentored and Robert to be his mentor. As she drove home that day she offered up a prayer to God to make this mentorship a reality. Kyle was seated at the kitchen table writing what appeared to be a letter when his mother came in the door.

Kyle looked over at his mother and without so much as a "hello" he told Avril that he would be open to being mentored. She smiled in thanks giving that her prayer was answered. She then asked Kyle what he was writing. Kyle smiled and handed the letter to his mother and said, "Mom this is for you." Reading the hand-written letter, it was a thank you to her for being the best mother in the world. Just then, all was right in their world.

Chapter 5

Mentor and Mentee

Robert visited Kyle and Avril at their home on Saturday morning with the meeting between them very pleasant and with just enough conversation to call it cordial. Robert asked Kyle quite a few questions regarding school such as his preferred subjects and his favorite teachers during his first two years in high school. Kyle was anything but enthusiastic and offered little insight into his educational likes and dislikes, but it was a good start.

Avril wanted to interject comments during this first meeting, but Robert openly suggested that she let Kyle be free to talk for himself without influence. Kyle liked that little gesture of putting his mother in her place. Avril got the message as the remaining time was spent allowing Robert to inquire, listen and learn all he could about Kyle.

At the end of this get together, Robert suggested that the first few times Kyle would meet with him would be spread out, a few weeks apart, so as to provide time for reflection by both of them. Additionally, it was decided that their mentor-mentee get-togethers would be after school, not on weekends.

Robert had grown up fast in his life as he was surrounded by people who made wrong choices, leading to lives of crime and desperation. Robert understood the barriers of building trust between two people and the fragility of maintaining that trust.

Robert was of the opinion that trust begins to develop by

listening, not by offering unsolicited answers to problems or speculative projections into the future.

Effective mentoring is a building process. You can't rush it or demand preconceived results. Every mentor-mentee relationship is unique and that is one of the reasons some mentoring match-ups don't work. Robert explained to Avril in their first meeting that there was no guarantee there would be a synergy between Kyle and him.

Robert's plan for, and with Kyle, was a methodical one of listening, and the first rule of listening is to be silent.

Throughout the early fall of Kyle's junior year in high school, Robert and Kyle might sit relatively silent for ten minutes of so and then take a short walk. Periodically, Kyle would ask Robert about his background and family back in New Jersey while Robert inquired about mundane school topics like homework assignments and cafeteria food. It was all part of the first steps in building trust.

Chapter 6

Suddenly

The rain that was falling outside of the school that day seemed to place a din over the normally free flowing chatter and atmosphere of the daily beginning of school. Students were showing the remnants of the driving rain that pelted the windows of the corridors that morning, tracking wet shoe prints and frizzy, aimless hair was the unintended style. It seemed a bit more cramped than usual in the eight foot hallway. One could hardly breathe in the humid air as the rain continued to fall.

Kyle was doing his best to move along to his third period class situated on C deck without bumping into everyone proceeding in the opposite direction. The pace of students moving along slowed somewhat and Kyle had become tucked behind two rather large boys. There was some laughter ahead and Kyle figured that a student performed some spontaneous act like falling down, precipitating the hallway traffic to come to a halt.

He could not peer over or around the two wide-bodies in front of him, so Kyle just played invisible and stopped for a moment. Not doing much more than looking down, the students in the crowded passageway began to budge forward.

Suddenly, with an abruptness akin to the lights being switched on in a darkened room at midnight, Kyle's eyes were transfixed on the face of a girl the like of which he had never seen. In a pure instant, he gazed at the most perfect of faces and Kyle's process of taking in air was in distress. He slightly raised his head, tipping his forehead back as if to position his eyes to see higher for surely this face was of heavenly origin.

Despite Kyle's normal comportment of never looking at anyone for too long and never with eye to eye focus, he could not turn his eyes from her and he could not imagine how anyone else could.

Moving closer, walking in the opposite direction she never looked in Kyle's direction. She was in a conversation with two other girls but did little more than nod her head. As he stayed almost flush against the corridor wall he all but consumed her every facial feature. Kyle's head was on a swivel, but his body could not move. Other students pushed by and into the slightly built Kyle. A few students bid Kyle to "get moving", but he could only strain to watch this girl as she disappeared into the mass of student bodies ahead.

As the corridor thinned to a few, Kyle stood motionless against the wall, his chest heaving as if the world had all at once been deprived of air. He turned to head to his next class, gathering his thoughts, and momentarily forgot his destination.

He entered his assigned classroom, arriving at the precise moment that the late-bell blasted its deafening sound. His teacher, Mr. White glared at the almost tardy Kyle, raising his index finger to indicate his vacant seat in the front row. Whatever Mr. White presented in lesson or text that day, it had nary a chance of entering Kyle's senses and certainly not his memory. He looked aimlessly ahead, not reacting to instruction or surrounding student response.

Kyle labored to remember every feature of her, then shaking his head in self-rebuke for not being able to recall each detail. This caused Mr. White to ask if he, Kyle, did not agree with the interpretation of the Shakespeare passage that was the object of the day's lesson. Kyle shrugged in response that brought a smirk from the girl seated next to him. An M-80 might have gone off under his desk that day with no response. Kyle was somewhere he hadn't been before and didn't know where that was. A sickly stirring filled his stomach, a new nervousness that as the years would go on, Kyle would come to know well.

Chapter 7

Discovering Perfection

The 20 minute walk home from school in the rain was spent thinking about this girl. Kyle recounted every second of the time she came into his gaze, passed by and vanished in the sea of students. Despite the briefness of looking at her face, he remembered a lot, but not nearly enough to sustain his need to learn more about her. Kyle felt foolish as he did not even know her name, and there was no one he could ask to tell him even the slightest details about her, let alone her name.

Once home he said little to his mother that night. Kyle was totally out of his routine. It was like he had been moved to a different life all because a girl walked by him. When Kyle's mother placed dinner in front of him and took his hand in prayer that was their daily pre-meal ritual, Kyle was unable to pray. His mother looked at him and asked if he felt alright. Kyle just stared back at his mother as she placed her hand on his forehead in a motherly act in checking for a fever. He looked at the food on his plate and moved it around with his fork, but there was no hunger, no want of food. Kyle lingered at the kitchen table for a few minutes, wanting to talk to his mother about what had happened that day, but he just didn't know how to explain. He went up the 3-step staircase to his room and sat down on the edge of his bed. In a few minutes Kyle's mother called up to him to ask if he wanted to watch television, and Kyle shouted down that he had homework to do. There wouldn't be any homework done this night as

Kyle didn't bring any home and besides he was totally pre-occupied with THE girl.

He tried to sleep that evening but found himself lost in thought, just rewinding those short few seconds of looking at her. Kyle felt lousy inside and could not seem to clear his mind. He decided to get up early the next day, get to school and look for her. All Kyle wanted was just one more look to know she is real.

Once at school, an hour earlier than usual, he looked down every hallway, and watched the buses unload their students. Kyle peered into every group of students as they gathered in the school foyer, in front of the auditorium and the cafeteria, but no sight of her. He felt more alone and isolated than usual, but all he could do was go through the motions, lost in his thoughts of her.

It was a Thursday that meant he had a study hall in the cafeteria during the next to last period of the day that was a bit of a walk from his biology classroom. Feeling tired from a lack of sleep from the night before and the disappointment of not finding THE girl, his eyes still stayed on the alert for her as he walked close to the windows on the way to the cafeteria.

Kyle never could understand the study halls. All students wanted to do in study hall was find someone to talk with and horse around. "Such a waste of time", he thought.

Once inside the spacious cafeteria, Kyle could not find but a few empty seats and they were next to seniors. The study hall monitor motioned him over to a seat at the far side of the cafeteria near the bagged up trash from the lunch waves earlier that day. With head down, Kyle took the only seat available, the last seat on the corner of the table.

Reaching into his worn book bag he pulled out his math book and decided to attempt to do some homework. All at once, as he turned to place the book on the table, there SHE sat across and just to his left. Kyle's eyes filled up with her. He stared … knew that he was glaring at her … and couldn't help himself.

THE girl was right in front him. Kyle's stomach seemed to be moving up inside his body, making his heart beat faster and faster. She didn't look at Kyle and just kept talking quietly to a girl, seated to her left.

Kyle couldn't rip his eyes from her. He wanted to memorize everything about her, every perfect part. Her eyes were as precious gems and there was no name of a color that could describe them. They weren't brown ... grey or ... blue. They were just perfect. She wore no makeup, at least he didn't think so, but her forehead, eyebrows, and eyes all fit in perfect order. She smiled during her conversation with her friend, as her eyes became gleaming crystals that surely could melt any heart, capturing anyone's soul. Her hair was as her eyes, of a color and texture all her own.

In another sudden moment that caught Kyle in mid breath, her friend pointed to Kyle and THE girl was now aware that he was staring into her magnificent face. THE girl let out a giggle with her friend that would have been most embarrassing except for the fact that her laugh was too amazing for words. THE girl spoke to Kyle with a simple, "Hi, you ok?" All Kyle could do was nod his head one or twice. With that, she introduced herself. "I'm Denise. What's your name?"

He could not respond. Kyle peered into her face and thought how perfect her name, D E N I S E.

Denise persisted, "so who are you"? Kyle could not break his eyes from her. This time, her friend interceded, "Can you talk? Do you have a name"?

Kyle's thoughts were no longer his own. He responded, "Denise".

Both girls broke out in muted laughter over the boy sitting across from them who was of special needs or on chemicals.

Kyle became immediately embarrassed, gathering himself, saying his name for them.

There was a sense of paralysis about him. He wanted to move and couldn't. Whatever the two girls said to him or about him, Kyle could not talk. He looked at the wonderful shape of her face. Oh, how her jaw line framed her devastatingly beautiful face.

Kyle wanted to touch her hair to feel those straight shoulder length silken tresses that laid so perfectly on the edges of her cheeks and onto her elegant neck. The fleeting minutes sitting before her, he kept repeating her name in his head. "Denise", he thought was there ever a more perfect name for a perfect girl?

After a few giggles at his expense, the two girls just ignored his presence, but Kyle's eyes continued to roam to every corner of her face. In some new manner of his thinking, he absolutely knew something had changed in his life and he never would be the same again.

The study hall monitor broke up Kyle's state of discovery by loudly announcing that all students should gather their belongings because the bell for the end of class is about to sound.

As Denise placed a few items back in her bag her friend applied her lipstick. Clearly, Denise, this perfect Denise, needed no such touch-up.

Both girls got up to leave and as Kyle raised up from his chair, Denise smiled at him. That drove Kyle right back in his chair. Unable to turn his head from her as she walked away, he noticed her walk, her legs, her behind and wondered if he would remember all this about one girl.

Chapter 8

Places Made Perfect

As Kyle exited the school for the 20 minute walk home he was consumed with the mental re-run of study hall, sitting across from the girl who now had a name, Denise. He repeated every recalled second, archiving her every feature in his head so as to never forget a single detail. Not a single strand of her dark straight hair required a brush to be repositioned on her head. He recalled a piece of scripture he heard in church that he and his mother talked about some time ago relating God's work ... and now, dazed by this girl, Kyle reached for an application of that scripture to her, ... "she was made with God's perfect hand, making her perfect".

Arriving home, he sat at the kitchen table and continued to ponder what had happened that day. He searched the memories of his short life and could remember nothing, no occurrence, that had shaken him to his core. Usually alone with his thoughts whether at school, around a few people or in the quiet oneness of being at home, waiting for his mother to come home from work, Kyle could not come up with anything that so captured his total attention.

He thought about where she might be right this minute. Was she talking with friends? Was she smiling at someone? Was she lighting up a darkened room by just walking in? This was nuts, he thought. What's wrong with me?

Kyle wanted to keep thinking about her, but then again he wanted to stop thinking of her. Was he losing control? Kyle felt his own face as it was warm. Maybe he was coming down with an illness that could be it. Kyle pulled the math book from his book bag and attempted a vain effort to do his homework.

Maybe this would be a good time to call Robert, his mentor. He quickly dismissed that notion. He had just started meeting with him and Robert would probably think he had a mental problem. Maybe he could talk to his mother about this girl. Never, he thought. Mom would ask too many questions. Kyle was used to solitary thinking, so this thing that just buried itself in his mind today would have to stay there without sharing it. It was safer he thought and maybe by tomorrow morning it would be all forgotten.

Avril came home visibly tired from her second job around 8:00 pm. Kyle noticed and offered to make her a sandwich for supper, but all she wanted to do was go to bed. As she kissed him goodnight and headed for her bedroom, she turned and asked, "Anything happen at school today"?

In just that instant, Kyle almost poured out the wonderment of ... sitting across from this girl named, DENISE. Then taking a deep breath, he tucked his thoughts back into his head, lied, and said, "... no, nothing happened".

Chapter 9

Returning to the Scene

For reasons known only to his heart, Kyle hurried off to school the next day and made a beeline to the cafeteria. At the cafeteria door, his eyes scanned the mostly empty room for the exact table where he sat across from Denise. Spotting it, he walked to the exact chair on which Denise sat and placed his hands on the back of the chair. It was as though that chair had been made perfect just because she sat there.

He saw the corridor outside the cafe filling with students and Kyle knew it was time to get to homeroom. Flashing the thought ... *maybe* Denise would be walking there in the corridors or sitting in the window seats along the halls. Instantly, he wanted to rush all around the entire school and search for her, just to catch a glimpse of her. Kyle had never felt as he did now.

With all the inner chaos he was experiencing, Kyle went to his classes, and tried to listen to his teachers. However, the one major difference, for the first time he was genuinely distracted. In the past, he could be thoroughly disinterested or bored, but this was more than different.

Kyle was habitually observant. He characteristically kept his chin in his chest and kept walking, but that didn't keep him from noticing what other students did and said. He didn't miss much but was careful not to react to anything he witnessed.

As if by magic the chance face to face meeting with Denise in study hall changed something. It wasn't long before Kyle realized that this one 40 minute period changed ... just about everything for him.

He looked for Denise. He wanted her to appear everywhere and as the days became weeks, he did see her in school. He never said hello and Kyle did nothing to make himself visable to her as she might say something to him. He noted everything she did when he did see her. Each time his eyes found her among the throngs of students his breathing became different. Sometimes when catching a brief sight of her he unintendedly held his breath for a moment.

About a week after their encounter Kyle saw her sitting along the window seats, leading to the library. He was over 20 feet away, but his "Denise radar" locked onto her. He froze in his steps, afraid to get any closer. He inched nearer, staying clear of her line of sight, but peered into her face. She spoke to two girls seated to either side of her, tilting her head as she listened. Her eyes opened wide and her mouth formed the words that he was too far away to hear, but Kyle drank in every facial gesture as if meant for him. Denise sat with elegance as if she was perched on a queen's throne. Kyle thought that the window seat upon which she sat should never again be filled by anyone else. Denise had, by her very presence, made that spot perfect.

Kyle's abrupt halt in that strategic place in the hallway so he could see Denise, hopefully without being seen, made him a human obstruction on the tile passage way, so other students had to go around, through or over him to get by.

The thinly built, but growing Kyle was as a stalled bumper car as students ran into and brushed against him to proceed on their way. He held his ground, maintaining his view that was more a stare at the magnificent Denise.

Slowly, he moved closer, just enough to improve his view, but not draw her attention to him. Kyle gazed at her as she spoke as Denise took in air and exhaled. So lovely and different than anyone in the world, he was sure. It occurred to him that maybe she breathed different air. Kyle studied her eyes. How they glistened and glittered like the aftermath of a firework, following the sound of the big boom. Her eyes were a voice unto themselves and he longed to sit across from her once again just to listen to her eyes. Yes ... Kyle could not find anything but perfection in this girl, Denise.

Over time Kyle would come to see Denise standing in classroom doorways, and walking throughout the school. As long as she didn't notice, Kyle would try his best to stand or walk in the exact same places Denise did so as to share the surface with her. These little locations and points of the school building, because she had stood upon them, were places now made perfect ... as Denise was, and always would be ... perfect.

Chapter 10

I Have to Talk About Denise

Kyle met with Robert at their usual Tuesday time and place, just to the left of the high school's main entrance. It was the first time that they had met since Kyle had that earth-shaking study hall, sitting across the table from "the girl".

Robert had talked to Kyle over the phone twice since their last meeting of two weeks ago and he sensed that something might be laying heavy on Kyle. It was nothing Kyle actually said. Rather, it was in the manner he talked as if he was watching a TV show while on the phone with Robert. The intuitive mentor asked Kyle if he was alright and Kyle, rather than answer with the one or two word responses to most any question replied with, "Of course, what do you think? One day, same as all the others. Is there a problem on your end?"

Robert was slightly taken aback by Kyle's almost irritable retort. He let this telephone moment fade but if Robert didn't know better he would have thought it was a girl issue, but since they started meeting, Kyle never expressed any particular interest in fairer gender, so Robert steered clear of the subject.

Kyle and Robert sat on one of the benches outside the school as the mentor got right into a discussion of Kyle's school day. They talked of a language arts project that Kyle was assigned along with the standard perimeters of subject, due date, and required length. As always, Kyle did not waste words and answered Robert's questions with short phases or single words. Kyle had begun to trust Robert, but their dialogue albeit on the phone or in person was devoid of embellishment or emotional flavoring.

As the 45 minute to an hour session was moving to a close, an unanticipated moment for Robert occurred. From out of the blue, Kyle sheepishly asked, "What do you do when you feel something, something you can't explain, ... about a girl?"

Robert looked off into the parking lot, not wanting to make eye contact with Kyle. This type of question was not uncommon for most young guys but from KYLE?

After what seemed like a lengthy pause, probably not more than a few seconds, Robert offered up a general response so as not to embarrass Kyle and take this conversation into an area neither was ready to go. "Kyle, is there a girl you have started to like?"

Kyle answered quickly, "no no, just a girl, you know, just a girl, but she is a little different."

Robert couldn't resist following up, ... not this time. "So, Kyle, what makes this girl different, you know, just generally speaking?"

Kyle was pushed back on his rhetorical heels. He didn't raise his eyes to Robert. He made some faces to himself, crunching up his nose and drawing one side of his face up and then the other, but no answer came out of him. He didn't know quite how to answer, or even if he should.

Kyle, jerked to a focus by Robert's "girls are girls" reference; snapped his eyes to Robert pointedly proclaiming in a very un-Kyle manner ... "Robert, you can't believe this girl. She's one of kind. Ahhhhhh, like something from another planet. You can't understand, you just can't."

Robert pursed his lips not wanting to laugh or even smile at Kyle's explosion of emotion. "Ok, I get it. You don't have to explain."

Now, the preverbal cork was out of the bottle and Kyle had more to say. "Robert she has the most amazing face and you should see her eyes. They are not green, not blue, not brown. They are like shiny grey, but they sparkle so much and when she looked at me I felt like I was getting a sunburn. You know what I mean?"

Robert could no longer hold back a smile. In the few times he had met with Kyle, he had never seen him so alive in his words. Trying to remain in the exciting moment of this unique conversation, Robert folded in with the description of her eyes.

"So tell me, Robert asked, her eyes were not blue, not brown, not green. Is that right?"

"Right", Kyle confirmed, "but they are this kind of grey. I'll bet no one in the world has her color eyes."

"I think people call the color you are describing as hazel," explained the mentor, Robert.

Kyle, now pumped up, uncovering something new about this girl, thought for a moment and barked out, "Yea, yea, I think that must be it. HAZEL eyes, hazel eyes".

Robert, not wanting to cap this conversation too soon looked at the now engaged Kyle and asked, "So ... does this girl from another universe with hazel eyes, have a name?"

Kyle's mouth dropped open at the thought of uttering her name. "Robert, you will not believe this. Not only is she like something else ... can't describe it ... totally different. She has this name. It's amazing just to say it".

Robert pushed forward. "So what is her name?"

"Robert, her name ... and you won't believe it ... is ... DENISE!"

Robert was baffled at the drama that Kyle affixed to this girl's name. In the brief time he had known Kyle, nothing or no one had caused him to speak and act so enthusiastically. It was as if this girl had ignited a fire in him. Robert hoped that this Denise, whoever she was, would only be a positive for him, but if this was a "crush", the first, he feared he could be in for a long rocky ride of emotions that Kyle was ill-equipped to navigate.

Chapter 11

Study Hall ... "Denise" Hall

Study Hall in high school met but once a week and since that momentous soul-shaking study hall period, Kyle counted the hours until the next study hall in the cafeteria.

His biology class preceeded the study hall period and Kyle was first out the door when class ended. As a boy who rarely hustled along for any reason, the thought of just seeing Denise again made him Jesse Owens. Kyle wasn't first to arrive at study hall, but he was of the first to stake out the same table where he sat across from Denise. He stood and wondered if she would return to the table and if she would even remember talking with him.

Kyle stood by the table and scanned the two large doorways to the cafeteria to catch any sight of Denise. As the study hall tables began to fill up, a few students came to the table and just sat down, he quickly pulled out the chair where Denise had sat the previous week and placed his book bag on it so as to signal its unavailability.

Just then, SHE walked in ... but she was holding onto the arm of a guy. His stomach leaped at seeing her but it was accompanied by a sickly feeling as she walked and laughed with his boy. It seemed that no matter what he thought or saw when it came to this girl, Denise, it was all new and unpredictable.

Denise, the boy, and a few girls entered the room, walking

in and out of the symmetrical rows of cafeteria furniture to the table that he seemed to be guarding. Denise spotted Kyle and with her entourage in tow and took the seats at the table. Kyle lifted his book bag from the seat she occupied last week as Denise took a seat at the end of the table next to the boy.

As Kyle seated himself the boy got up and said, "Hey, I'm going to sit over there with the guys."

Denise raised her eyebrows and with some measure of sarcasm, said to him, "Good, I wanted to talk to Kyle anyway".

Kyle, caught off guard by even being mentioned by her, turned his face to her in disbelief and uttered, "You remember me"?

"Of course", Denise casually noted.

With that acknowledgement, the boy who was leaving the table, stopped and looking back at Kyle with scorn asked, "and who's this ... never saw you before."

Kyle retreated to his shy shell and did not answer, but Denise did.

"Frank, this is Kyle", Denise stated as if introducing a younger brother to a friend.

Frank glared at Kyle and with condescension dripping from every word, "Kyle huh, and what is a Kyle? You go to school here? Never saw you before. You a foreign exchange student?"

Again, Kyle did not respond and kept his eyes on the table before him.

Denise bothered by Frank's sense of rudeness raised her voice and snapped at Frank, "That was cruel. Why don't you go hang out with your guys."

Demanding the last word Frank countered, "I'll leave you to your geek". With that Frank touched Denise's hand and told her, "See you at the gym before I go to practice."

The other girls at the table looked at Denise with some embarrassment on her behalf as one of the girls, asked, "Why do you put up with that stuff from him"?

Kyle kept his eyes down and heard her reply, "... because I love him."

Kyle remembered the discussion he had with his mother

that touched on "love", but the way he was made to feel at the moment and the word Denise just uttered, made him confused.

The girls changed the subject, talking of some event they were attending on the coming weekend as Kyle searched his book bag for anything to do. Kyle was not talked to for the remainder of the period, but every so often he would look down the table and captured a glimpse of the incomparable Denise. Kyle thought about the comments that Frank had directed towards him and it was not the first time he had been subjected to such hurtful words by other students. It was one of many.

As the study hall was coming to a close, Kyle thought about how extra special the study hall of last week had been and how crappy this one was.

With just a few minutes left in the period, Denise got up from her seat, coming over to his left. She knelt beside him. All at once, he was close to her, a closeness that made his heart thump in his chest. As she knelt, he was inches from her eyes, those incredible eyes and for the first time noticed a tiny line near her right eye. That line instantly became a part of the vividness of all things Denise.

Kyle wanted to just touch her hair and face. They were so close. Kyle felt as if his chest was coming apart. He looked into her eyes and hoped she did not see him breathing so hard. Knelling, Denise placed her hand on his shoulder and it was as if God was touching him.

Denise began to talk, … no … Denise began to whisper … to him. At least he thought it was a whisper.

Kyle, she began, "I want to apologize for …".

Just then the bell for that change of classes sounded.

"I can't be late, Algebra 2 test. Give me a pen", Denise demanded.

Kyle handed her his pen. With that Denise wrote what appeared to be a phone number on his book bag.

"Listen", Denise rushed to say, "This is my phone number. Call me tonight."

"You want me to call YOU?" … a disbelieving Kyle asked.

Denise hurriedly exited the cafeteria, looking back at a stunned Kyle, yelling out, "Call me, OK?"

Kyle did not answer. He grabbed up his book bag and looking at the phone number that Denise had written, he headed to his next class.

Chapter 12

Word Ways to Love

As Kyle headed home at the end of the day, he relived the study hall period when the negative feeling caused by the comments of that guy, Frank, were turned to exquisite happiness by Denise. Being called out and embarrassed were all worth it as Denise asked <u>him</u> to call <u>her</u>. Kyle had never called a girl before in his life with the exception of his mother. He thought how amazing this all was. How could this have really happened? Denise asked him to call her.

When Kyle arrived home, shortly before 3:30 pm he looked at the kitchen clock and considered, so what is the right time to call Denise? Oh my God, he thought, she didn't say a time to call. He didn't need this pressure!

His mother would not be home until after 8:00 pm after her second job, so it seemed like a good idea to call her at 7:00 pm.

Kyle would agonize, counting the minutes, until 7:00 pm but there was no guarantee that Denise would be there. What if she was on the phone with someone else? He considered what he might say to her, what she might ask him ... and then he remembered what his mother had told him some time ago, ... just find your ways to love. Kyle remembered one of the ways to love was just to listen. Kyle would not admit to himself that he loved Denise. That would be silly.

The hands of the kitchen clock seemed to move very slowly that afternoon. It was 5:30 pm, the time he usually made something for himself to eat, but he had no appetite this evening. His stomach was nervous and he was feeling nauseous. Could this call to Denise be causing this lousy feeling? There was no denying, this enchanting girl, was making him feel this way.

At 7:00 pm ... he picked up the receiver of the digital landline telephone that sat on the kitchen table. Slowly, he dialed every number, applying a little more pressure to the number keys, so as not to misdial. Kyle took a few deep breaths.

The last number being pressed, he waited for the sound of her cellphone ringing. Three rings passed and Kyle nearly hung up.

Then there was a "hiiiiiiiiiiiiiiiiiiiiiiiii" being spoken. Kyle answered back, "Denise?"

"Yes, ... hello", the voice on the other end responded, "Who is this?"

Kyle, unsure of the right way to talk on the phone to Denise, replied, "This is Kyle. You told me to call you, remember?"

"Yes", she answered.

He waited for Denise to begin some kind of conversation. Kyle felt he was a mass of "duhhhhhhhhh" and didn't want to sound like a jerk.

Denise spoke softly in the most incredible sound he had ever heard over the phone. Her voice was a delicate wisp of sound like the fluttering of a hummingbird's wings. It was a private voice, meant only for him. The words had a sparkle to them, just like her eyes. He caught himself breathing faster now. Was he really talking to Denise?

"Kyle, I wanted you to call me, so I could apologize for how you were treated today in study hall", explained Denise. "What was said to you was rude and we all knew it", she continued.

For the first time, Kyle wanted to say something. "Denise, you did not do anything wrong. It was that guy you were with. Why are you apologizing to me?"

Denise continued to explain. "Frank can be kind of tough on people with his mouth, but he really is a great guy."

Kyle's first impression of Frank was anything but proof that he was a great guy.

"Denise, can I ask you something? You don't have to answer."

The velvety voice on the other end rolled out a sensitive response, "Kyle, you seem like a nice boy, so you can ask me anything, but I may not have an answer."

Kyle knew what he wanted to ask, "Who is Frank?"

That one question, those three words, were about to open a flood-gate, resulting in years of discourse.

Denise explained that Frank was her boyfriend and she "had been with him" since they were in middle school. "He's really a great guy and he is sooo cute. Don't you think?", Denise giggled.

That question ... "Don't you think?" caught Kyle off guard. Was she really asking me if I thought he was cute?

Before Kyle could get another question out, Denise continued her verbal resume of Frank, "He plays on the football team and I love watching him play. He wears No. 89 and he should have been captain of the team, but the coaches have their favorites."

Despite the topic, Kyle was reveling in just listening to Denise. Kyle wanted to ask a question and hope it didn't sound lame.

"So, what kinds of things do you like to do in school?" Kyle inquired.

Denise began, "I'm a senior. Are you a freshman Kyle"?

Kyle told her he was a junior and Denise reacted with surprise, "Really, I've never seen you around school."

Kyle thought about how invisible he must be to people in school.

Denise told Kyle that she had been a cheerleader and was class president last year, but wanted to concentrate on other things during her senior year. Then added, "Frank never liked me being a class officer and that always hurt because I liked being in a leadership role."

Kyle being careful not to say the wrong thing, asked, "So, what are your plans after high school?"

Denise hesitated to answer, "Well, of course, I want to go to college, but I'm not sure where. Frank wants me to go where he goes to college, you know, kind of do it together. Hey, want to hear what Frank did last summer?"

Although Kyle's heart sunk a little every time he heard her say the name Frank, it was what Denise wanted to talk about, so Kyle encouraged her to continue.

Denise very anxious to tell the story began, "Last summer we broke up for a while. Frank was being a jerk and I found out from my girlfriend that he went out with another girl. I was so hurt cause I love him so much. Anyway, my family went up to the lake for a vacation week. Frank and I weren't talking, but he drove all the way to the lake to apologize to me. Isn't that the most romantic thing you ever heard?"

Kyle, hardly used to hearing about relationships of any kind, and certainly would not know what is considered romantic asked, "So everything was alright after that?"

"Well of course. He's so wonderful," she boasted. Denise continued to talk about Frank in many ways, referring to him as everything from cool to funny, from popular to sometimes mean.

Kyle's mother got home around 8:20 pm and was surprised to find her son on the phone. Avril smiled and bending over in front of Kyle's face, squinted her nose and jerked her head up as if to ask, "who is it?"

Kyle waved to his mother not to interrupt him, as Avril smiled and left the kitchen. Kyle began to realize that he had been on the phone way over an hour. It was the longest phone conversation of his life.

Kyle was in a new place in his life. He was having a talk with a girl that made him think about her in endless ways. He didn't want the conversation to ever end.

Finally, Denise stated, "Kyle, you are so easy to talk with. I could talk to you for hours."

If ever a compliment made Kyle beam, this was it!

Kyle enthusiastically responded, "Denise, I really like listening to you. You can call me anytime you want."

Denise asked for his number and Kyle did not hesitate to

give it. She entered his home phone on her cellphone. Denise told Kyle that she had to go and then hastily hung up. It was an abrupt ending to the long call, but it was another time that he would never forget, made possible by this one totally different girl, Denise.

Upon hanging up, Kyle's mother came dancing down the hallway from her bedroom to the kitchen and with hands on her waist, loudly asked, "Now young man ... who was that?"

Kyle trying to appear something akin to "cool", said soberly, "... just a girl"?

"A GIRL?", shot back Avril and then repeated the question, "A GIRL"?

Kyle felt it was time to just give his mother just a little information on this girl as she was too magnificent to keep a secret. So Kyle provided a muted, brief description, although he wanted to raise the roof to explain this unequaled example of human perfection to his mom.

"Mom listen please", Kyle opened, "This girl is off the charts in every way. She's nice to me. Her hair ... her nose ... her chin and her eyes, oh eyes ... her right eye has this little line ... her voice."

Avril understood what Kyle was describing. She recognized the symptoms from her youth. She saw what was in his eyes as he detailed the girl in less than 60 seconds, but Avril was just pleased to be sharing this with her son.

Avril, exhausted from the end of her two-job work day could only smile and listen. Her love for her son always spread out in terms of recognizing potential consequences when she learned of things going on in his life. Over the years there hadn't been much in Kyle's life to get excited about.

She knew instantly ... Kyle was experiencing a new thing, a crush.

Just as Robert had asked him in their last meeting, Avril simply inquired, "What's her name"?

Kyle covered his mouth with his left hand, and moving his head back and forth as if he was about to disclose some secret of the ages, spoke her name with reverence, ... DENISE!

His mother getting a little playful with the moment, restated, "Her name is Denise, really"?

Kyle, thinking that his mother heard something magical in her name just as he did, answered, "MOM, have you ever heard a name so incredible in all your life"?

Avril fought off a laugh, so as not to dampen her son's joy and excitement.

It was now time to get some organization back into the waning hours of the day. Avril asked if Kyle had eaten anything and her son acknowledged that he wasn't hungry, another symptom that Kyle was somewhere in "crushville".

His mother took a few steps to the tiny kitchen and began to prepare something to eat for both of them. As she removed some leftover chicken from the refrigerator, she pondered the word, "crush". She learned long ago that a puppy love is called a "crush" because there is a long emotional road to travel from an apparent physical attraction to a more meaningful feeling of adoration that makes the individual very susceptible to the stings and pain that come with love, resulting in sometimes being CRUUUSHED. Avril had been there, but she knew there was no way to prevent her son or anyone from having to deal with the results of a "crush".

Chapter 13

Phone Friend

Kyle did not see Denise in school the day after that first phone call, not that he didn't look for her. Kyle's head was on a swivel throughout the day to the point that his neck started to hurt. He was disappointed that he didn't even catch a glimpse of her, but he did see Frank twice and each time he had this bad feeling about him. He wasn't sure what to call it, but Kyle did not like Frank in any way.

Upon arriving home from school, Kyle got right on his homework. He did no homework the day before because he was waiting to call Denise and sure didn't do any after the call because his head was too consumed with rethinking the call.

Kyle had a sandwich that his mother left in the refrigerator for him and he ate it as he worked on a science paper that was already overdue.

It was just after 6:30 pm when the phone rang. Kyle picked up the receiver thinking it was probably his mother telling him that she would be late tonight. Answering he heard that special voice say,

"Hiiiiiiiiiiiiiiiiii".

Over the coming months, the first word Denise spoke was always this elongated, "Hiiiiiiiiiiiiiiiiiiii". It was her signature first word.

He was instantly filled with such a joyous feeling. He thought that no one could make him feel happier than just by hearing Denise talk.

After the "long hi", Denise started the conversation with … "can you talk"?

Kyle answered with an excited, "YES"!

Denise wasted no time in asking Kyle, "Do you know what Frank did today"?

Kyle didn't answer, because of course, he wouldn't know, and Denise got into telling him this story about how Frank was holding her hand today. As they were holding hands and walking past the main office with a lot of other students around, Frank pushed her hand aside and told her she had greezy palms. She said she felt so embarrassed. How could Frank do this to her?

Kyle knew enough not to offer any comment and just listen.

For the next hour, Denise mixed in complaining about all the things Frank does to annoy her with how much she loved him. It was all confusing, but one thing was becoming clearer to Kyle. He didn't like Frank and could not understand how he could do anything to hurt this wonderful girl, Denise.

Over the next two weeks, Denise would call Kyle, except on the weekends. It was always around the same time of day, 7:00 pm, so he managed his after school day to make sure that he wasn't doing anything else, including homework, eating or sleeping when her call came. At the end of most of the calls, Denise would tell Kyle that he was a good listener and told him she'd talk with him the next day.

In each and every phone call, the topic got around to Frank sooner or later. Kyle never felt put upon or bothered by this. He kept remembering his mother's words … "find your ways to love". He just accepted that all he could do for Denise is listen. His feelings about the perfect Denise kept growing stronger and he was developing the need to protect her, another first for him.

Kyle would see Denise in school, although not every day. Sometimes she would just wave or smile and others Denise would not notice him at all, but Kyle relished every time his eyes found her. Denise and Kyle only talked in study hall, but that was only for a few moments as she was always talking with her girlfriends or Frank.

41

Avril was becoming a trifle concerned about her son and this girl that she knew so little about. Avril knew that they talked on the phone almost every night, and one evening, his mother suggested that he ask Denise out on a date. Kyle immediately squashed that idea, explaining that Denise had a boyfriend who she was in love. Avril was perplexed by the amount of time her son spent on the phone with Denise, even though Denise seemed to have no interest in anything other than a talking friendship with him. As much as Avril wanted to inject more motherly advice to her son relative to this first heart-throb, she decided to let this relationship just play itself out.

The telephone friendship between Kyle and Denise continued throughout the fall season, into the winter months and the holidays. The only thing that changed was an increase in the length of the calls and sometimes multiple calls in one night. Periodically, Denise would call after 9:00 pm. Avril would sometimes answer the phone when a call would come in late and Denise was always polite, asking to speak to Kyle and apologizing for phoning so late. Despite her feeling that this phone friendship might be getting out of hand or there was some deeper issue involved, Avril stuck to her belief that it would all run its path to conclusion in time.

Chapter 14

The Art Project

Kyle's art appreciation class was interesting and his teacher, Mrs. DuBon, required that two projects be done during the half year course. The first project assigned was a comparison of artistic styles by local artists. This required that Kyle and all the other students had to find the time to walk around the art galleries on North Prince Street. Not that Kyle had any conflicts in his otherwise home existence on the weekends, but it just seemed like such a boring endeavor, until he happened to spot that girl, Denise, walking there with one of her girlfriends on that particular Saturday morning. Avril had dropped Kyle off at the end of North Prince Street with a clipboard in hand to make his written comparisons on the form provided by Mrs. DuBon.

Kyle hadn't walked long along the 100 block of North Prince Street when he spotted who he thought was ... Denise. He thought ... I could not be this lucky. No, it couldn't be, but it was her. This was the first time Kyle had ever seen Denise out of the school and he wanted to watch and absorb every part of it ... without being seen. He hurried along and positioned his walk approximately 20 yards behind Denise and her blonde female companion.

If Kyle was motivated to study bipedal locomotion ...walking (as an assignment in school), he might begin to view walking as something of an art form. Kyle considered that most people take walking for granted, but on this one day in Kyle's perception of the simple act of walking changed forever.

Less a matter of pace, nor destination or purpose, Kyle was fascinated by the walk of one amazingly flawless girl, Denise.

Kyle could not recall ever being drawn to watch another person walk before Denise chanced before him. She was a tad more than five foot, measured against the geometry of Kyle's diminutive height. Appearing before Kyle on the long sidewalk of North Prince Street, Kyle walked behind Denise and her friend on this day that inserted yet a new wedge of wonderment he had never previously known about her.

What immediately garnered his attention was how her body flowed in perfect synchronization. Denise's shoulders were a perfect straight-line parallel to the ground on which she walked. As he watched from maybe 20 yards away there was never a dip or drop of either shoulder. Even when talking with her friend as she walked, her shoulders seemed to remain so motionless.

Walking paces behind her, Kyle stumbled more than once on the uneven sidewalk of North Prince Street. He could only hope that she would not turn around and notice that it was him. Kyle was self-conscious enough staring and starry-eyed at this pristine girl, the like of which had no peer in his eyes, so he didn't need to embarrass himself further by being acknowledged for his now, puppy dog behavior when it came to Denise.

Some people have a tendency to swing their arms across their body when they walk as if their hips require additional propulsion to move their legs. The arms of this incredible girl that moved before Kyle just grazed her hips with each step. Not too much movement back and forth, nor too little as if the arms were meant to be nailed to the body in some sort of robotic maneuver. No Denise's every move was utter perfection.

If it was just her upper body alone, that would have been enough to burn a marker on Kyle's life memory. However, her legs were so faultlessly proportioned it was if the Italian Renaissance artists had used her as their one and only model on which to craft their historic masterpieces.

While Denise's friend walked at her side with a typical asymmetrical teenage gait, Denise walked as if there was only air beneath her feet. Denise flowed in her steps and floated forward, seemingly to fly if she so willed.

Not the passing of loud-engine cars or the bustling crowd could draw Kyle's attention away from her walking. All at once, Kyle noticed that he had unintentionally increased his pace and was closing the gap between Denise and him. A similar moment occurs when one is trying to read the bumper sticker or license plate on the car in front of you and the next thing you know you are tailgating.

Immediately checking his stride down to an almost stop, he was taken by Denise's hair that flew backwards in his direction from the breeze that blew to her face. It glistened and glowed with a texture that was unique to only her. The morning sun had to have been designed just to enhance her hair. Kyle had been close to Denise's hair only twice, but now, more than ever, he wanted so much to just touch the silken tresses that draped her face and neck. If there ever was the slightest thought to the contrary before now he was certain that no other girl could ever match Denise's perfection?

Chapter 15

Defining Denise

As the holiday season approached, the traditional activities of the school year moved into full swing. The Homecoming Dance, Pep Rally, yearbook photos, and the voting for senior class superlatives were part of the annual schedule of school activities that Kyle hardly gave a passing thought through his first two and a half years in high school, but this year was different, all due to Denise's presence in his life.

The nightly phone conversations had become deeper in recent weeks as Denise shared her dreams for the future, her opinions on many topics, as Kyle was content to be her sounding board in listening delight. No matter the time, the topic or what Kyle had to do, his world stopped for Denise when he heard her voice. Although the largest chunk of conversation was usually about Frank and the things he did to bother and hurt Denise, Kyle was there for her with no selfish intentions or agenda.

Kyle learned so much about Denise through these phone conversations and his admiration grew for her. He discovered that although she was beautiful, smart and popular, she didn't want to be a center of attention. Denise was motivated to do good things for other people and always first to volunteer for public service activities in school.

Despite her endless vitality and character, Kyle began to see her as vulnerable. He worried about how easily she seemed to be bruised by things students would say and do, especially Frank. It bothered him that he could not protect her.

One evening after a call from Denise, where she described a nasty verbal attack by Frank as he accused her of not paying enough attention to him, Kyle sat at the table, looking forlorn. His mother, seeing Kyle not in his usual joyful state after talking to Denise, asked him if he was alright. Kyle explained to his mother that he worried about her and wished he could do something to guard her against the slings and arrows of what others (Frank) say to her.

Avril felt privileged that Kyle opened up to her about Denise who he never discussed with anyone. His mother put her arm around Kyle and said, "Son, you are a good friend to Denise. She feels safe with talking to you. She trusts you. Whether you realize it or not, you give her a place to feel safe just by listening. Remember what I told you about finding your ways to love? Well, you are giving of yourself to her, loving her in your own way."

Kyle rearing up at any mention of the word *love*, looked at his mother with clear dissent, "Mom, who said anything about love."

Avril gave Kyle a look with raised eyebrows as if to say, "... oh really?"

Not wanting to continue this conversation with where it seemed to be going, Kyle kissed his mother and headed off to his room to bed.

Chapter 16

Christmas Gifts

As people began decorating their homes for the holidays, the talks over the phone between Denise and Kyle were sprinkled with Denise asking Kyle's opinion on gifts she wanted to purchase for Frank. Kyle had grown to dislike just the sound of that name, *Frank,* but he would listen as always and give an ambiguous hard-hearted answer if pressed.

One evening, Denise enthusiastically explained, "Kyle I have a great idea for a gift for Frank. Tell me what you think. I want to get a baseball cap for him with the school logo on the crest of the hat and his football jersey number on one side and his initials on the other."

Kyle remained silent for a few seconds as he made an ugly face into the table lamp, thankful that Denise couldn't see him through the phone at that moment.

For the first time, he was tempted to say something negative to Denise about anything. Never one for witty comebacks, Kyle held back, but responded, "It sounds like a good idea, won't cost you too much, I'm sure the most important thing is to get the right size hat for him".

Kyle jumped out boldly in the conversation with Denise and asked, "What do you want for Christmas"?

"Oh, my parents always give me a lot of stuff and I am sure Frank will give me something", said Denise.

Kyle would not let his question go and asked again, "Denise, what do <u>you want</u> for Christmas"?

Denise asked, "Why do you want to know"?

Caught in a question that required his total candor, Kyle responded, "Denise I want to give you something for Christmas".

"OK", Denise went on, "I want you to continue to be my friend forever".

Totally caught off guard, Kyle responded with his heart, "I will be your friend forever", a statement, a declaration ... a commitment that he would never relinquish.

Denise not appreciating the depth of what Kyle had just said inquired, "And what do you want for Christmas?"

Kyle didn't hesitate, nor did he consider any options, "May I have your graduation photo?"

"Sure, if you really want one?" Denise answered.

As their phone call came to a close, Kyle's mind was afire with thoughts of getting something for Denise that would say, "...a friend forever".

Chapter 17

Lead with Love

Christmas was a quiet holiday for Kyle and his mother. They only had each other so there were never a lot of gifts as Avril despite working two jobs, never had much extra cash on hand. Avril would put up a small artificial tree in the corner of their living room and on Christmas morning there was a hand full of gifts under the tree for Kyle. A few weeks before Christmas, Avril would give Kyle an envelope with whatever cash she could spare. With that money, Kyle would purchase a gift for his mother. This year Avril gave Kyle $23.00 in the envelope.

With the joyful arrangement between Denise and Kyle to exchange gifts, there was a feeling of frustration as Kyle knew he would not have money to purchase a gift for Denise unless he used some of the cash his mother gave him. Kyle knew he couldn't do that. His mother was the most important person in his life and beside he already had something in mind to buy his mom.

Once again remembering what he had been taught by his mother, "find your ways to love", Kyle considered how he might find something to give Denise. He hadn't done much in his life, didn't own much. He had asked Denise for her picture, but he had none of him to give her, not that she would want one anyway. Kyle didn't have a clue what to do. Getting desperate, he decided to call Robert, his mentor.

As he entered the numbers of Robert's cellphone, Kyle was trying to figure out the best way to ask Robert for an idea for a gift for Denise. Even though Robert knew about Denise, Kyle always felt that he acted like a goof when her name came up.

Kyle explained the circumstances and Robert, calm and cool as always, asked Kyle if he wanted to borrow ten dollars to go get her a gift. Kyle thought for a moment and then realized that even if there was money, he hadn't a notion of what he might buy her that would mean something to her.

Kyle expressed to Robert his frustration at not knowing what to do, what to give Denise.

Robert suggested various inexpensive things such as a keychain with her initial, a charm with her name that she could wear with a necklace, a small doll, or a Christmas ornament.

With Robert out of practical ideas, he suggested a path that seemed very much like the teaching Kyle's mother had imparted some time ago. Robert offered this advice, "Kyle, in all things in life, you need to lead with love. If you are confused and don't know what to do next, ask God for help and start with love. Remember always, your love is the best part of you ... it never fails, it never wears out. Your love is continually new and fresh, so lead, start your ideas with love, an answer will come to you."

Kyle stayed silent as Robert spoke, hoping to hear a quick solution.

Sensing that Kyle was all over the place in his thinking, Robert proposed, "Kyle, why don't you <u>make her something</u> that comes from your heart?"

"Like what", snapped, Kyle?

Robert wishing to be patient in helping Kyle find an answer, "You care about this girl, probably more so than you will admit to me or anyone, even yourself. Why don't you make her something with your own hands? Write something for her. You can do it. What are you afraid of ... let your feelings out a little?"

Kyle, getting the idea that Robert might be getting impatient with him thanked Robert for his time and suggestions and ended the conversation.

Kyle sat quietly for a while at the kitchen table and then

went to his bedroom that he promised his mother he would clean that day. Hanging up some shirts in his closet that his mother had cleaned and laid on his bed, Kyle noted the presence of a shoe box that contained a pair of dress shoes that he hated to wear. The box looked new with no markings, except for a sticker with his shoe size.

Kyle started to formulate a gift idea. Maybe he could make something of the shoe box that would be creative enough to make Denise smile, without her laughing at him.

Looking at the shoe box from every angle, he noted the rectangle shape, especially when turned with the narrower sides on top and bottom. What if he created a "shadow box" like the ones students employ for projects that include photos and memorabilia?

The question ... what to put inside the shadow box?

Then it hit him right between the eyes.

He would try his hand at writing a poem.

He had tried to write poetry in language arts class when he was in 7th grade. He wasn't very good at it, but maybe this time, for Denise ... he could do it.

It was two weeks before Christmas and there was no phone call between Denise and Kyle where the mention of exchanging gifts came up, but for Kyle, it never left his mind. Each day he worked on the poem. He would write a few lines, tear them up and start over. It was getting close to the holiday and this was a single opportunity to actually meet with Denise and give her a gift. The real gift to him was just being near Denise. Denise was the gift he wanted.

As Kyle worked daily on the poem with every spare second and more, he prepared the shadow box (shoe box). He made it as ornate as he could with ribbons and cut up pieces of old birthday cards his mother had stored in a bag in the garage. From an old couch pillow, he cut off the tassels and attached them with crazy glue to the four inside corners of the box.

Kyle was afraid to show his mom or Robert the poem he was writing, but he did know that the kind of poem he was writing was called an ode.

From his English class of last year, he remembered that

an ode is a type of poem devoted to praising a person or event, and it is usually written to express deep feeling. Well, he thought, if ever there was a poem with deep feeling, this was going to be it. It might turn out to be the worst ode ever but he was committed to doing his best for Denise.

One evening, a week before Christmas, Kyle was determined to finish the poem that night no matter how long it would take him, regardless of how corny it may turn out to be. He did not answer the phone that night, knowing well that he missed a call from Denise. He tried to make every line mean something special to him, not only Denise. He wanted the ode to be about the brief time they had known each other and hope that it would mean something years from now. At approximately 2:00 am the poem was done.

He took the hand written poem to school the next day, planning to type the poem over in school after classes and print it out in the computer lab. There he could select a fancy font, center the poem on the screen and print it out. He read it over and over, finding fault with it each time he read the stanzas.

Chapter 18

It's Not What You Give, ...

IT'S HOW YOU GIVE IT

Two days before Christmas, Denise called as she always did during the week.

Uncharacteristically, Kyle took control of the conversation from the start, "Denise, a few weeks ago we agreed to exchange Christmas gifts".

Denise had all but forgotten about that conversation and the idea of gift giving between them, but immediately recalled that Kyle wanted a graduation photo of her. "Yes", she answered, "Sure let's do that tomorrow. Does that work for you?"

They both agree to meet right after school in the back of the school library. Denise, not knowing what Kyle might be giving her, thought the quiet and generally empty tables at the back of the library would be a good place, away from the nosey friends of hers.

After saying good night over the phone, Kyle was on a mission to complete his shadow box and then wrap it with last year's Christmas red and green wrapping paper.

He gently trimmed the paper that the poem was printed on so it would fit the rectangle shape in the bottom of the box. Looping scotch tape in a circle, he created his own double face tape, placing a loop of tape in each corner. Then with great care, Kyle pressed down the poem into the box until it was firmly fastened.

After one last look at his workmanship, Kyle placed the lid on the shadow box, and taped the cover on securely. The somewhat worn wrapping paper of a year ago was just enough to wrap the shadow box.

Kyle took one more precaution just in case he dropped Denise's gift or some student would accidentally bump into him holding it. He wrapped it in a hand towel, emptied his book bag and placed the package in the book bag. This was one day he was leaving his books at home. When he arrived at school, Kyle stored the bag, encasing Denise's gift in his locker where it would be safe from harm.

Now, the challenge for Kyle was HOW to give the gift to her. His plan no matter how silly it might be was to take the wrapped box out of his bag, take a knee and present it to her like she was the queen of England. The *how* included him saying, "my Lady, a gift from common Kyle".

The day dragged on as he counted the passing classes and hours until he would meet with Denise. Kyle looked for her in the hallways as he always did, but on this day he wanted only to see her alone with him in the library at 2:30 pm.

As school came to a close, Kyle returned to his locker to retrieve the book bag. He faced his open locker as if hiding something and looked into the bag one more time to make sure nothing had happened to the Christmas present. With that he clutched the book bag against his chest, closed his locker and made his way to the library, arriving at 2:25 pm.

The front of the school library from the hallway was one of floor to ceiling windows, so Kyle could peer into the room to see if Denise was there before entering. Looking through the windows, left and right, front to back, he saw that she had not arrived as yet, so Kyle decided to find a table at the back of the library and wait.

Standing by the table in the farthest left corner he turned to the front so he could see everyone who came into the library. Minutes started to seem like hours as he waited and thought about how he would just say hello. Although he would often wait up for his mother to come home from her second job, it did not prepare him for waiting on The Girl, Denise.

Kyle's already nervous stomach was joined by a dry mouth and a propensity to keep swallowing.

Kyle kept looking up at the clock at the front of the library. At 3:00 pm Kyle first considered the possibilities ... maybe she's not coming ... maybe something happened ... maybe he got the wrong day.

Just then he saw Denise outside the windowed entrance. She was with Frank and they were not smiling. Frank's right hand was pointing in her face and he seemed to be yelling at her. Kyle considered walking to the entrance to say or do something to stop this apparent argument, but abruptly, it ended as Denise pushed open the library door and entered alone.

Denise walked slowly to where Kyle was standing. As she came close, Kyle saw that her eyes were full of tears. The sight of those amazing eyes that Kyle had come to worship, so terribly unhappy, made his heart sink in shared pain. Kyle stepped towards Denise with the intention of maybe hugging her, but Denise turned away from him and dried her tears with a tissue she took from her bag.

Kyle did not know what to say to Denise. He felt that his words, whatever they might be, would just sound dumb at that moment.

Denise seated herself at the table, looking down at the table top, still mopping her eyes with the tissue.

Kyle discerning that this might be the wrong time for gift-giving offered, "Denise, I don't know what just happened and I know it is none of my business, but maybe we can meet and exchange gifts another time."

Denise, radiant even through tears, looked up at Kyle and motioned for him to sit. She forced a smile and said, "I wish you didn't see that. Frank can get emotional at times, but he is ok, really".

Chapter 19

It's Raining, ... Of Course, It Is

With that Denise rose from her chair and said, "Kyle will you go for a walk with me"?

As if Kyle could ever say no to Denise, they walked out the back door of the library, down the long hallway to the rear doors of the school. Quietly, Denise and Kyle, the same height, walked with synchronized steps as if they had practiced walking together. Denise was the first to notice their aligned stride and asked, "Kyle, are you trying to walk just like me?"

Kyle not exactly sure what Denise was talking about asked, "I am doing something wrong?"

Denise starting to cast off the unfortunate incident with Frank, began to smile and responded, "No silly, but you and I are walking with the same steps as Buckingham Palace Guards."

Kyle looked down to see for himself, stumbled, and almost tripped over his own feet. Denise instantly, broke out into the most genuine laugh, saying, "Oh Kyle, I am so sorry. I didn't mean to laugh at you."

Kyle smiled, overjoyed that something he did would make Denise smile after being so tearful just a few minutes ago.

Kyle still pressing his book bag to his chest containing Denise's gift, held the door open for Denise as they exited the school. They walked the long path through the tall trees towards the elementary school some quarter mile away. Kyle asked, "Denise where are we going? You know, it's supposed to rain this afternoon."

Offering no words of a destination, Denise just said, "Don't worry I won't let you melt."

The skies were overcast and the first few drops of rain began to fall on them as they walked slowly together. Kyle's heart celebrated in this moment of just walking with her, but he was tense and Denise knew it.

Denise casually mentioned, "So Kyle, did you say something about exchanging Christmas gifts? I think I recall you saying something about that."

Kyle looked over at her wondering if she meant what she just said.

Denise showing a playful side of her that Kyle had never heard over the phone led them both to just smile at each other. At that moment Kyle was feeling this new kind of happy. He thought ... she is magical to be able to make me feel this way. At the same time, he had learned that Denise was very sensitive, capable of great joy, but easily hurt.

The dark skies might have indicated snow if not for the unseasonable moderate temperature, but rain was coming. In passing, Kyle mentioned to Denise that they might get caught in a heavy rain if they didn't turn back soon, but the light-spirited Denise remarked, "Kyle do you think I will look so icky, drenched from the rain, that you will run away from me?"

Kyle confronted with the first question ever directed at him that could be construed as "teasing", responded with stark innocent honesty, "Denise? ... How could anyone ever run from you?"

Denise cocked her head to the left with a coy smile, and joked, "Kyle ... Are you flirting with me?"

"NO, no, no, I'm not, ... honest, I'm sorry," panic-talked an embarrassed Kyle.

As the wooded pathway wound its way to a clearing, there at its center was a natural rock formation, known as "Traver's Table", named after the farmer who found the oddly shaped rocks. Two flat surfaced boulders were pressed together to form a "V" contour. The "table" was approximately three feet high and eight feet across.

Upon arriving at "Traver's Table" Denise suggested they sit on the angled rocks facing each other at its apex. Now sitting perpendicular to each other with Kyle's left leg almost touching Denise's right leg, Denise confided the reason for the argument outside of the library with Frank. She explained that Frank wanted her to go to a holiday party with some of his friends where alcohol and drugs would be present. Denise told Frank that she refused to go and it sparked the argument. She apologized to Kyle once again and asked that they change the subject.

The rain increased, making the rocks appear slick, but Denise made no suggestion for them to leave.

Kyle was enjoying this time with her so much that a hurricane might not have prompted their departure ... at least from his point of view.

They both were beginning to be well wet on their hair and shoulders, so Denise suggested that they begin their ... "little Christmas together".

Kyle thought to himself ... maybe it would be a good idea just to loan Denise his book bag with the gift in it and let her open it at home.

Kyle voiced his concern, "Denise, because of the rain, why don't you take my gift to your home and open it there. Just take it home in my book bag."

With that, Denise showed some surprise, asking, "You have a gift for me in that book bag?"

Kyle replied, "Well of course I do. Thought you wanted to share gifts with each other?"

"But Kyle", Denise cautioned, "I am only giving you a picture of me like you asked. What are you giving me that requires that it be covered by your big book bag?"

Kyle smiled back, reached into his bag and took out the wrapped Christmas gift. Handing it to Denise, whispering, "Merry Christmas Denise," droplets of rain fell on the wrapping paper, causing the colors of the paper to run. Kyle tried to shield the package with the empty book bag, but the rain began to intensify.

"You better not open it now with the rain. Take it home," recommended Kyle.

Denise now curious to see the gift, "No, I am opening it now."

With the enthusiasm of a young child, Denise ripped the wrapping paper off the box, and seeing the recognizable shape of the box, concluded a question, "You got me shoes?"

Kyle burst out a laugh as the heavens opened and they were caught in a torrential downpour. Try as he might to cover her head and the gift with his book bag he could shield her from the rain and wind. Denise pulled off the cover of the box, dropped it on the ground, revealing the shadow box with the poem. Denise asked, "What is this?"

Kyle seeing his creation dampened by the driving rain could only say, "It's for you."

In a matter of seconds, he was shattered with disappointment, wanting his gift to Denise to be so special, now the paper on which the poem was typed and the box itself was soaked by rain.

Denise grabbed the box's lid off the ground, trying to cover the gift, but it was too late to prevent the rain damage. Kyle's gift was a mess.

Denise looking at Kyle saw the disappointment in his face. As they both sat there getting totally drenched, Denise asked, "Kyle I am very sorry everything got so messed up. What is in the shoe box you wanted to give me?"

Kyle, almost on the verge of tears, shyly provided a description of his Christmas gift to her. "I wanted to give you a gift that would give you special smiles now and maybe in the future. I decided to make you a shadow box with a poem I wrote for you."

Looking into Kyle's eyes, inches from his face she uttered, "You wrote ME ... a poem?"

Kyle looked at her and sheepishly shook his head, indicating yes.

Denise covered her mouth with both hands and began

to cry again, wondering how she could have been so casual about his gift that led to it getting saturated and falling apart.

"Kyle, no one has ever written me a poem before," Denise confessed, "I can't believe you did this for me."

"I am so sorry for making such a total mess of everything you did."

Kyle tried to ease the guilt Denise was feeling, "I will make you another copy of the poem. It wasn't much anyway; just something I tried to write for you."

As the rain pelted down over their faces, Kyle held the waterlogged box with both hands.

Denise reached out, touched Kyle's face with her right hand, sending a chill through him.

"Please Kyle, please, would you read it to me", Denise spoke softly?

"You want me to read the poem ... to you ... now," replied Kyle?

Denise smiled and repeated, "Kyle, please read me your poem."

The rain, heavier than just a few minutes earlier, had all but obliterated the typing on the page. Kyle showed the interior of the box with what remained of the typed poem to Denise. Kyle looked at Denise's face through the lens of his heart, her rain soaked hair lying straight down against her face with beads of water streaming from every glistening strand. She was more beautiful than ever and he longed to tell her so but kept his words to himself.

Kyle cast aside the cover and held the remains of the typed page before his eyes as a corner of the page ripped off from the weight of the water. He looked at Denise and admitted that the paper was too badly damaged to just read from it. Kyle closed his eyes for a moment and realized that after all those many times he read and re-wrote the poem, then typed and retyped the poem, he had it memorized.

Once again he asked Denise, "Are you sure you want me to read this to you?"

Denise shook her head yes, and quietly asked, "Kyle does the poem have a title?"

"An Ode to Denise," said the drenched Kyle.

"Now, read it or say it to me," all but commanded Denise.

Kyle slowly stood up from his seat at the rock table. His hands held fast to the disintegrating piece of paper that he tried to spread out in his fingers, keeping the paper from folding in the wind. He looked into the hazel eyes of the seated Denise who was looking right into his face and recited the poem, never once looking at the paper.

AN ODE TO DENISE
by Kyle

Dressed in blue, a double hue
Of cobalt and textured old navy.

I couldn't look away, you made my eyes stay
Who was this girl in the hallway?

Though postured and slight, an elegant delight,
Each movement your statement of beauty.

In my stomach butterflies, your hazel eyes did hypnotize,
They spoke words that gave off no sound.

Your lips velvet shine, that whispered sublime,
Breathing air only meant for Denise.

Each night when you call, I become ten feet tall,
Just listening to the magnificent Denise.

So Christmas is here, now one thing is clear
I can't give you all that you want.

Pure as you are, the very best by far,
I'd give you the world if only I owned it.

Forever your friend, you are my godsend,
Whatever you ask I shall do.

Your folks give stuff, but not nearly enough
To tell you how much you are loved.

No Santa am I, but forever I shall try
To be your forever best friend.

Kyle spoke the words of the Ode to Denise. As they looked at each other, Denise's tears were indistinguishable from the rain that continued to fall upon them both. When he was done, neither could speak. Kyle crumpled up what was left of the paper and tossed it on the ground. Denise picked up the discarded lump of paper, put it in her bag and said, "I want to keep this."

Totally soaked and shivering, Kyle and Denise began the walk back to the school. Denise began to say something once, "Kyle, I want to ....," but her voice cracked and she sobbed. Kyle looked upon her a few times as they walked back in the rain, but was unable to unlock the words he had tucked in his heart. They just would not come out.

They re-entered the high school as Denise called on her cellphone for someone to come pick her up.

Kyle wanted to wait with Denise for her ride to arrive, but Denise insisted he should go.

There was so much Kyle wanted to say to her if nothing more than just to ask if she liked the poem. Kyle lingered with her as long as he could when he saw that the ride Denise called for had pulled up and it was Frank. Kyle turned to leave as Denise softly said, "...call you."

Kyle wanted to look back at Denise, but on this day, after all, that had happened; he did not want to see her ... with him.

A million thoughts and feelings surged through Kyle as he went back into the rain to walk home. As cold and wet as he was, he really didn't care. He wanted to cry but couldn't. He wanted to run back to Denise and say something more, not knowing what or how. He had a sense of failure in a way he had never known.

The manner in which he wanted to present the gift to Denise with a little humor and maybe a hug never happened. Instead, the GIFT he gave was somehow changed by HOW he gave it. Rather than have the quiet back table of the library, the "how" turned out to be the sounds of rain and wind, and the shared shivers from the chill. Yes, the gift was changed by the HOW. He thought about what Robert had once imparted to him, "It's not the gift it's how you give it". Maybe someday he would be able to control the HOW, but today his gift was inalterably something different that one he had planned. He hoped that Denise would remember it fondly.

As he neared home it occurred to him that Denise never gave him her photo. Kyle smiled and realized he had been given a gift after all ... another meeting with DENISE.

<u>What could ever be better than that?</u>

Chapter 20

Avril Recognizes "The One"

When Kyle arrived home, he stripped off his soaked clothing just inside the front door, so as not to track water all over the place. Changing into anything dry with a towel over his head, he sat at the kitchen table and recounted each little moment of that afternoon with Denise.

Sometime between 5:00 pm and 7:00 pm he fell asleep, face down, at the kitchen table. He was awakened to the sound of his mother coming into the apartment, grousing about the rain that continued to fall outside.

Seeing her son laying on his arms at the kitchen table, Avril came to his side, asking if he was alright. Kyle's first thought, upon shaking off the cobwebs of his impromptu slumber, was Denise. With grogginess still filling him, he moved his eyes around the room as if looking for Denise.

Avril, with her mother's intuition kicking in, took a seat next to her son. Something seemed very out of the ordinary about her son at that moment.

Kyle felt an urgent need to talk to his mother now. "Mom," as he began to cry, "Something happened today that I don't know if I can really explain to you."

With that Kyle described how he wanted to give Denise a Christmas gift and how he created a shadow box with a poem inside. He also apologized for cutting the tassels off the pillows on the couch.

He detailed the events of how he *wanted* to give the gift to Denise and then what actually happened. Trying to hold back his emotions, the origins of which he did not understand, he told his mother, "Mom, I was alone with Denise. Can you imagine? We walked together, just her and me. It rained hard and it didn't matter to us. She looked at me and I looked at her and we hardly said a word, but it felt like we were saying a lot to each other. Mom, do you understand what I'm talking about?"

Avril, smiling at her son, "Son, I know what you are talking about."

Kyle continued, "I feel sad, but I am happy. I want to cry and I want to smile all at the same time. Mom, I wrote Denise a poem and I don't know how I did it. It just all came out. You know what else? I sat with Denise, right next to her and after a few minutes, I wasn't nervous anymore. And Mom, the most amazing thing of all ... I never tried to memorize the poem. You know I have the hardest time memorizing stuff for school and I really try. When the rain ruined the page with the poem, Denise asked me to say the poem to her and I remembered every word and I was looking at her the entire time. Mom, I don't understand what happened."

Avril was watching her son grow up right before her eyes and it was time for her to impart some reason to the confusion of his heart. She began, "Do you remember the conversation we had some time ago about, "There is only one".

"Yes, mom, I do."

"Well it's time to tell you another part of that piece of truth," confided his mother.

"Finding "the one" doesn't necessarily mean that this is the girl you get to marry, or even spend a lot of time with. No, it is far more than that. "The one" is a person who brings out the best in you ... someone who makes you feel that you are capable of anything in life. What's remarkable about her is that she doesn't have to be right next to you to do any of this."

Avril continued, "Once "the one" has brought forth something from your heart, mind, and soul that you never knew you could do or ever thought you could be ... it will remain with you forever. Kyle, what happened today is that Denise instilled in you the confidence that you can become anything you want to be, achieve any great thing and most importantly, that anything is possible."

Kyle listened intently, "Mom, you really think she did all that with one walk in the rain?"

"Yes son," Avril extolled, "You see, Kyle, Denise is probably "the one" for you. I have encouraged you, always loved you, but no one has ever gotten you to do the things that this girl apparently has and my guess is that she always will."

Kyle was on overload. There was so much to understand from today, but it was time to slow it all down and have dinner with his mother. Avril got up from the table with the impression that her son was on the verge of a new era in his life ... and whoever she was, she thanked God for Denise.

Chapter 20

The Picture

When the morning arrived there was a cold chill in the air and although the skies had their clouds, there was no rain in the day's forecast. Kyle dressed quickly for school and bore a new kind of attitude, one of anticipation. He really was looking forward to the day, even if he didn't spot Denise in school, but somehow he knew he would.

The first few periods of the school day flew by and his science teacher, Mrs. Welch remarked to Kyle, "Oh you are smiling today." Indeed, there was joyfulness flowing through him and he knew that what Denise and he had shared, coupled with his mother's explanation of the event, was putting some steam in his step. The entire day felt so new in so many ways.

Just after the fourth period, Kyle took a detour to go to his locker to pick up his math book. Out of the crowded hall, he heard a yell, "Kyle, wait up." It was Denise running towards him, out of breath, panting, "I've been looking for you all day. I have to give you your Christmas present, can you meet me after school in the front foyer?"

Kyle gave a wide smile to Denise and bashfully stated, "... but Denise, it's not raining!"

Denise with those flashing eyes, cocked her head to one side as she had done before in front of Kyle and demurely responded, "It's ok ... we'll make believe that it is."

When school ended Kyle bolted to the school foyer and this time Denise was waiting for him, leaning against one of the brick beams of the lobby area. She was dressed in a white collared blouse with a sleeveless sweater over it, but Kyle hardly noticed much more than her faultless face.

Kyle stopped right in front of her, their eyes leveled before each other. Denise smiled and in the same fashion as their telephone conversations always started she said only, a long "hiiiiiiiiiiiiiiiiii". Like so many things about Denise, Kyle was of the opinion that only she could say it ... wear it ... be it.

Denise reached into her bag and took out a brown envelope and gave it to Kyle. "So open it. This is your Christmas present."

Placing his book bag on the floor, Kyle carefully opened the envelope and took out the white and sepia (a reddish, brown standard color for many high school graduation photographs) photo of Denise. He looked at Denise ... then the photo ... then back at Denise without sayng anything.

A puzzled look came over Denise's face with the question, "Kyle, don't you want it?"

Kyle immediately responded, "I want this picture more than almost anything else you could give me."

"Ohhhhhhhhhhhhh," Denise inquired, ... and what do you want more that my picture?"

Kyle looked into Denise's eyes as she stood fast and didn't pull her eyes away from him.

He so wanted to answer her question. He could think of only one answer and it was so clear to him. Kyle deferred by saying, "Denise, I hope someday you will ask me again ... and if you do, I hope you like my answer."

"Other than having a few minutes with you," stated Kyle, "this is the best Christmas present I have ever received."

Denise just smiled at him, and almost apologetically saying, "I have to go".

Kyle stood there watching Denise walk away, noting her every movement, just as he had done during that morning when he was supposed to be working on his science project. He thought to himself ... "Is there anything Denise is ... does ... or can do ... that she doesn't make dazzling?"

Chapter 21

Denise Made
School Matter

With the holidays behind them, Denise entered the last few months of her senior year, but Kyle had found a new person, living in his body. Denise with thoughtfulness that was not much more than the sound of her voice and or the twinkle of her words brought meaning to Kyle's education. Unbeknown to her she had done a lot with little, but that was all that was necessary to instill in Kyle the belief that he mattered. He was important as a little slice of Denise's life. Without intention, Denise set free a teenage boy's essence that resulted in a surge of self-confidence with subsequent academic victory.

During the third quarter of his junior year, Kyle was a buzz-saw of energy, enjoying every one of his courses, asking questions in class to the point where his teachers would wave him off and ask, "Anybody but Kyle have a question?"

Kyle's third quarter report card was reflective of this new untethered young man with all A's and a particularly amazing A+ in mathematics.

Denise and Kyle would talk over the phone most nights but not as frequently as before the holidays. "Senioritis" had set in on Denise. She was voted "prettiest girl" in her class and she was making her final decision as to where she would attend college. Denise told Kyle that she was leaning towards attending the same college as Frank, a comment she made to him some time ago. She never stated a reason for making such a move, but Kyle had settled into a regular pattern of just listening without offering any inkling of an opinion.

The Junior Prom had come and gone during Kyle's year and he never even considered asking anyone. The buildup for Denise's senior prom occupied a number of their conversations on the phone and Kyle so enjoyed hearing Denise's enthusiasm for the selection of her prom gown, but swallowed hard with every thought that she would be escorted by Frank.

Kyle volunteered to work as a server for Denise's prom with only one motivation ... to see her in her gown. The gym was spectacularly decorated for the theme, "Dreamy Night of Delight". Kyle handing out punch and cake to each table let his eyes drink in the gown that Denise described in detail in numerous conversations. She was more beautiful than he ever could have imagined in that gown. Denise wore an embellished fishtail gown of pure silk with translucent elements and embroidered glimmering sequins from the round neck, down the long sleeves. Although Kyle had never danced with anyone before, he wondered what it would be like to dance with Denise, just once.

To no one's surprise, especially that of Kyle, Denise was voted "Prom Queen". How could there even be a second place, he mused?

Chapter 22

Ways to Love ...
Yearbook Patrons

The school year was winding down fast and Kyle did not want to imagine not seeing Denise in the high school next year or not even talking with her on the phone. Kyle fought hard not to think about it or even discuss it with Denise. She was all excited about college. Who wouldn't be? He did not want to say anything negative or selfish to her.

In this anxiety of possibly losing contact with Denise next year, if not sooner since her parents were planning to move out of town after her graduation, he decided to find a new "way to love". This led him to the idea of putting something in the yearbook that would tell Denise how he valued their friendship and no one, maybe not ever her, would ever know he had done it.

Kyle rarely asked his mother for money for any reason. He knew she had a plan for every dollar that came into their apartment. Every night Avril would carefully place loose change into covered glass pots and had made it clear that no matter the need, no change was to be taken from them. Kyle never violated that edict, but he needed a few dollars for his idea.

When Avril arrived home that night, much later than usual as she was working overtime to save more money for some reason, Kyle approached her.

Diplomatically he asserted, "Mom, you know I never ask you for money, but I want to purchase a "patron" ad in this year's yearbook."

"What's a patron ad", she inquired?

Kyle explained that a patron line or ad is a few words you write for the yearbook when you want to say something about a senior, a club, or an activity in the school like a sports team. Each patron line costs $2.00.

Avril looked at him straight in his face, "Son, the only reason you want to put a patron line in the yearbook is for Denise, ... and you know it."

They both laughed and Avril said, "The way your grades have skyrocketed, how can I say no to you? I think I can afford $2.00."

Kyle quickly corrected his mother, "Ah mom, I want to do more than just one line."

"Ok, how many ads at $2.00 a piece do you want to buy," pressed Avril.

Kyle thought about it, clearly not knowing yet the fullness of his plan, "I really haven't decided, but you will be first to know in a few days."

With that almost promise from his mother for financial support, the subject was closed for the night. Kyle would begin this creative endeavor forthwith.

Kyle set to work to write five yearbook patron lines. Each of these were Kyle's way of expressing something about Denise, just finding his ways to love.

Even if Denise never looked at these ads, Kyle would know he left something for her in her yearbook. The patron ad lines he wrote and bought for $2.00 each were:

Wetpoem4D
Dthanks4photo
Kforever4D
DKrain
RememberTT

Kyle realized that Denise would be off to college next year and he might not see her again for months or even a year, but maybe those five silly lines would remind her of him ... maybe.

Chapter 23

The Kiss

After the prom, there were an endless series of senior activities, ceremonies, and awards dinners. With Denise so immersed in everything, the number of evenings when Denise could call had greatly diminished.

On a Wednesday evening, Denise called Kyle, lacking the joyful "Hiiiiiiiiii", he had come to anticipate.

Denise began, "Kyle I need a favor. Please help me."

Hearing the need in her voice, "Denise whatever you need. How can I help?"

"Kyle, can you drive me home after school tomorrow?"

Denise knew that Kyle did not have a car, so this was more than a passing request. Kyle would have to ask his mother if he could borrow her car, something he had never asked his mother before. Kyle had his license and would run errands for his mother when she was home and the car was not in use, but taking his mother's car to school? That would mean Avril would have to get a ride from someone, probably one of her co-workers. To make matters worse Avril worked two jobs and would have to cobble some rides together from home to the first job, then one to the second job, and then one to home at night.

There was urgency in Denise's voice and for the first time, he didn't want to deny Denise in need, THE GIRL in distress.

Kyle made a quick end to Denise's call for a ride and called his mother at work, promising Denise he would call her back.

Calling Avril on her cellphone at work, an unaccustomed

occurrence, Kyle opened the call, "Mom, sorry for calling you at work, but I need a favor."

Avril seemed shocked in responding as Kyle never called her at work, "Kyle what's wrong?"

"Mom, let me come right out with it. Denise called me. She doesn't sound right. She asked me if I could drive her home from school tomorrow."

Avril had witnessed sudden and wonderful changes in her son in the last eight months, and she recognized that it was because of the presence of this girl in Kyle's life. They were friends. Avril had never met Denise, but Robert concurred with Avril that Denise was the one most responsible for Kyle's metamorphosis. This request as inconvenient as it was ... well, it had to be considered. This could be just another step forward for her son.

Avril had no plan, but granted the request, "Kyle, hear my words. You have never taken my car to school. You have never had a girl in the car with you, other than me. Do you know what you are doing?"

"Mom, I don't know what's going on with Denise, but she has never asked me for anything before ... anything!" I know this puts you out because you have to ask for rides to work and home, but mom I wouldn't ask if I didn't hear something like fear in her voice."

"Ok, ok ... you can have the car tomorrow, but you better be careful ... in every way you better be careful. Do you understand me?"

With almost tearful gratitude for his caring mother, "Mom, thank you."

Kyle called Denise back and told her of his mother's kindness in letting him have the car to take her home on the following day. Denise sniffling in tears, "Kyle I need to see you, talk to you. That's why I need you to drive me home, but I don't think I want to go directly home, ok?"

Kyle could only agree.

Denise, gave a short goodbye, "Kyle, I gotta go."

The next day in school, Denise was waiting for Kyle as he entered his homeroom, another first for them. Denise waiting for Kyle, something must be wrong? A somber Denise handed him a folded note that read, ...

"Meet me at the auditorium entrance with your car at 2:30 pm. Thanks, Denise".

Throughout the day Kyle was preoccupied with the anticipation of driving Denise home from school. Day after day he would watch the cars pull out of the full student parking lot, located near the gymnasium at the conclusion of school. He often wondered what it would be like to have a girlfriend and drive her home. Denise wasn't his girlfriend, but for one afternoon he might feel special just being in her company. Unfortunately, something of a hurtful or burdensome nature happened in Denise's life in the last few days that precipitated her call to Kyle for a ride. Kyle pondered with all of her friends and her boyfriend, Frank, there were probably many other people she might have asked for a ride, so why him?

With the school day over, Kyle headed for the parking lot and with great care backed his mother's car out of the student parking lot. He drove to the south entrance of the school near the auditorium. Kyle pulled over next to the curb and got out to find her, but Denise was already coming out of the auditorium door and walked rapidly to Kyle's car.

Kyle opened the passenger side door for Denise and found himself looking at her in a far different way than ever before. In any previous moments in school, his eyes were always on her face, especially her eyes that had become bejeweled magnets, fastening his gaze to them. Now, for the first, and probably for the only time, Denise was there with just him.

There was no entourage of friends and the bristle of spontaneous conversation. Most notably, there was no Frank, the guy who did not deserve to be Denise's *boyfriend*. After weeks of phone calls where virtually all of Denise's talk was about Frank, Kyle wondered if the conversation during the drive from the school parking lot to her home would be of Frank.

As Kyle held the car door for Denise, it did not surprise him at all that she stepped in and sat in her own unique way. Rather than step in and just be seated, Denise first sat on the edge of the car's bench seat closest the door and momentarily hesitated before swinging both legs simultaneously into the car. This elegant seating process drew Kyle's attention to Denise's legs. Instantly, Kyle found yet another wonderment of the fabulous Denise and his eyes followed her legs. This did not pass unnoticed by Denise as she titled her head slightly to her right, pursed her lips with a smile. Ordinarily, Kyle would have been caught a bit embarrassed by such a happening, but he just smiled back.

The interior of the car had instantly become transformed by Denise's mere presence. Kyle started the car and it occurred to him that he had no idea where he was going. Before putting the car in gear, he looked over at Denise (as if he needed a reason to look at her) and glibly asked, "Where to …?" Denise in an impulsive response of playfulness, unknown to Kyle, replied, "You got some place in mind?"

That question caught the naive Kyle off guard and he hastily answered, "I thought you wanted to go home." Denise released a laugh that Kyle had often heard on the phone and somehow it was more wonderful having heard it right there in front of him.

Denise gave directions to Kyle and he diligently followed each instruction. Denise said little else during the ride, and then asked if he was in a hurry. Kyle certainly had nowhere else he would rather be in the whole world than with her, even it was only to serve as her chauffeur.

Denise then asked Kyle to drive to Markley Street and get on Route 222. He could not imagine where she wanted to go. He only wanted to please her.

The radio was playing, but Denise remained rather quiet, only remarking about a passing license plate and a few random comments about other students who Kyle only knew by name. After driving for about 30 minutes, Denise told Kyle to take the next exit which led to long rolling hills of green farm land. Driving down a narrow country road, Denise stared ahead as if she knew exactly where she was going. Finally, with a sense of courage, he asked Denise to explain just where they were going. Sternly, Denise looked at Kyle and told him to pull over near the lake front on the left. Obediently, Kyle turned the car into an unpaved area as Denise told him to turn the car off.

For the first time in his life Kyle was alone with a girl, but not just any girl, THE GIRL.

Denise turned in the seat to face Kyle. Kyle could only sheepishly look over and try not to act stupid in anyway. Denise just glared at Kyle and disarmed him. Something was definitely on her mind and somehow he knew it wasn't good stuff.

Her usually joyful eyes all at once seemed burdened as if some weight rested right on her shoulders. Kyle peered into that lovely face whose every feature was studied and beloved by him. He looked at the narrow little line near her right eye and the slight up curl of her lower lip. Kyle thought every perfect thing was in its perfect place as she lifted the fingers of her hands to cover her mouth. With that her eyes closed, then opened, and streams of tears traced the smooth complexion of her face. She briefly raised her head with eyes closed and then dropped her chin to the top of the edge of her blouse, weeping uncontrollably.

Kyle lifted his left hand, almost reaching out to touch her arm, but pulled it back not knowing what was the right and proper thing to do.

He spoke softly to Denise with words that tumbled from his mouth. "Denise", he began, "are you in pain?" Denise's hands moved up over her eyes as her muted sobs spoke of some pent up anguish.

Denise pulled her hands from her dampened face and began, "Kyle, I can't talk to anyone about this. I tried to talk to my mom and dad, but I couldn't do it."

Kyle lifted the sleeve of his shirt to Denise to dry her tears. With that, she quietly said the name, "Frank". Kyle raised his brow as if to say, "...who else?"

That opened the doorway to Denise's tale. Expecting nothing and everything, Denise told Kyle that Frank had slapped her two nights ago and it wasn't the first time. What followed were a series of rhetorical statements that left Kyle to say only "oh no" and "I'm so sorry".

Denise kept insisting that she loved Frank and he loved her and that he probably didn't mean to do it. She blurted out, "I'm so scared. I feel so alone. I just needed to talk to you, but not on the phone."

Her usually joyful eyes all at once seemed burdened as if some weight rested right on her shoulders. Denise extended her arm and just touched Kyle's hand and her perfect eyes locked into Kyle's. Instantly, there was no thought of Frank and all the trouble that haunted her heart. There was just Denise, clearly, fondly, forever Denise.

The remnants of her tears lingered on her curved cheeks, and more than ever before there was a flawlessness to her every feature. Denise moved her face gradually closer to Kyle's face with her eyes never once leaving his. As if paralyzed by the very air she breathed, Kyle could not move his face, nor alter the explosion of his senses from the soft elegance of Denise.

Denise's eyes closed so softly as she placed her velvet lips on his. Kyle's eyes, wide open in awe and disbelieve, that this paragon of loveliness had just kissed him, quivered with a torrent of feeling never known, and never to be equaled.

She pulled her head back with a gentle smile and looked into his eyes. Kyle wanted to understand, wanted to place a name on what had happened, but there was only awe and wonderment.

In an instant of adoration, Kyle asked, "Denise? ... May I touch you?" Kyle did not know exactly how he wished to touch her, only that he did.

Denise did not answer. She only smiled with a casual movement of her head up and down. At once, Kyle did not know what he would do. He only knew he wanted to touch her and in some way make her feel that everthing would be alright.

Melding into her glance, now so close, so pure, so true, he raised his left index finger to her radiant lips. Trying to make this first touch light enough to tap a bubble without making it burst, Kyle placed the tip of his index finger at the middle of Denise's lips. His heart stopped and his breath seized to beat as the tip of his finger felt the velvety surface of her lips. The miniscule spot where her two lips meet were as no other texture could ever feel. How such a single point on the human body could be so perfectly positioned and adjured for just one touch was beyond the comprehension of young Kyle.

His finger paused on that poured texture of love and suppleness as Denise's eyes closed and her head titled back. Kyle could not resist the moment and never would again.

As if guided by the Hand of God, his finger moved along her upper lip, an outline of discovery and desire. Kyle did not understand the feeling or the motivation, but he slowly almost imperceptibly and lovingly moved the very tip of his finger along her lips.

Kyle felt his hand, his finger was not his own. There were no excess movements, just the steady touch of his finger. Denise did not move, nor respond in any way. She was one with Kyle in this "first touch".

When Kyle had fully outlined her lips and raised his finger from her tender mouth, Denise spoke tenderly ...

"Kyle, I don't know what to say now. I am feeling something different that I cannot explain. Will you do something for me?"

Kyle only whispered the word, "yes".

Denise continued with her eyes locked onto his ...."Kyle, would you please do what you did with your finger ... with your tongue?"

Kyle had just scarcely taken a glancing kiss from Denise moments ago and now THE Denise wanted something from him, he had never even contemplated doing.

He was helpless before her. He was lost in all that Denise was, and would always be, although he would not understand it for many years to come.

To that endless request, Kyle placed his face close to Denise, closer than he had ever been to anyone. He had no idea of how he might comply with her request, but try he must.

Denise was so beautiful and delicate to Kyle; he wanted only to be but a faint touch on her lips with his tongue, a mere feeling of a spring breeze on her lips.

With a loving effort of naïve touching, he parted his lips and extended the tip of his tongue on the right edge of her lips. The initial sensation was of feeling silken cloth on one's skin, but with an almost tingly energy that touched his every body part. Gently, oh so gently, he traced the softness of the edges of her lips as she heaved a sigh and her arms reached to hold his shoulders and then about his neck.

Kyle had no pre-determined idea of how he would complete this movement of affection, but he continued the gradual movement of his tongue along the somewhat swollen boundaries of her lips. There was no real beginning and no end. He touched her as she had asked, never asking Denise if he was meeting the measure of her request or fumbling about in his rank naiveté and innocence.

When he had outlined her lips a few times, he caught her quickening breath on his face. At once, he stopped for no reason. It just seemed right as everything had with Denise. He drew back his face from hers and just stared into her eyes.

No words were spoken. No smiles were exchanged.

Denise had talked to him in a whisper through his kiss. He felt something that touched him to his core. Denise's heart had talked to Kyle's heart. Denise without a word had forever more captured the heart of a simple, quiet boy ... and neither of their lives could or would ever be the same again.

They both knew it was time to return back to town, back to the reality of the present. The naïve passion that brought them to a place neither could have imagined hours ago left few words to be spoken. Something was kindled in Kyle's body, a fresh way to feel that Denise had shared with him.

For Denise it was back to the circumstances that made this day possible, back to parents she could not talk with when in pain ... and back to Frank for whatever lay ahead.

As Kyle pulled into the driveway of Denise's home, Kyle leaned toward her in a failed attempt to kiss her on the cheek as she departed. Denise had opened the passage car door and was almost out as she dipped her head back into the front seat and said, "call you."

Kyle would not receive a call from Denise that night, nor

would he for almost a week. He considered calling her but guessed she might be dealing with the problems with Frank, so he resigned himself to just thinking of her in a harmony of mind, body, and soul.

Chapter 24

It Only Takes One

The last semester of Kyle's junior year in high school brought still new heights of academic achievement, straight A's in all subjects, earning accolades from his teachers and end-of-year awards as the top algebra II student in his class and certificates of recognition in Chemistry and Language Arts.

The days were peeling off the school calendar far too fast for Kyle with few sightings of Denise during the school day. Denise would call a few times a week, but the talks were far too brief for Kyle. Denise informed Kyle that she would be matriculating to the same college as Frank. Kyle young, but of an evolving discerning mind, felt this would lead to no good.

Of particular lingering concern to Kyle was his wish that they would discuss the events of their time on Route 222. It had been such a powerful moment in time for him and he hoped that he was not the only one who felt that way. Denise never referenced the topic and Kyle, out of respect for her, never broached the subject either.

One of the last times, Kyle saw Denise in school was the day that the yearbooks were handed out. Kyle had looked everywhere for her so she could sign his yearbook and he hers. If ever there was one person he wanted to sign his book, Denise was it. Additionally, Kyle thought he would place a piece of paper between the patron's pages and just maybe she would see his secret notes to her.

Near the end of the lunch waves, Kyle spotted Denise in the auditorium lobby, surrounded by other students who waited for her to sign their yearbooks and share some casual hugs. Through the throng of people, Kyle and Denise made eye to eye contact as she whispered to him, "Hiiiiiiiiiiiiiiiiiiiiii iiiiiiiii". That velvet voice instantly melted his heart ... again. Kyle wanted to write in her yearbook what he really believed he felt for her and could never say to her in person. Kyle had it all planned what to write.

Kyle patiently waited for Denise to sign his yearbook, but as the bell sounded for the change of classes, Denise was gone in a wave of student traffic and never did get a chance to sign his yearbook. As it turned out it was one of the disappointments of his life.

Kyle was an honor usher for graduation that June and had an unobstructed view of Denise sitting in the front row with the other seniors who achieved a top ten ranking in the class. Kyle watched her receive a number of awards at graduation and applauded loudly after every one. As the ceremony ended, Kyle walked over to Denise in hopes of having a few words with her, but again she was inundated with friends and her parents, most wanting to take pictures with her. Denise broke away from the crowd for a second and said, "Thank you for being my forever friend. My parents and I are moving to Georgia next week. I gotta go."

Standing in dazed silence, Kyle stood there watching her walk with her parents from the graduation ceremony. The incredible sadness, not knowing if he would ever see "The Girl", Denise, again, was too much to fight back. Kyle began to sob and looked for a place he could hide so no one would see him.

Denise and Kyle would talk one more time before the end of June, but the two central topics were how hot and humid it was in Georgia and how much she missed Frank. Kyle tried to empty his heart in words in that phone call, but he never found the right crack in the conversation to tell Denise how much she meant to him.

Those words sealed deep inside Kyle would remain unspoken for many years to come.

Chapter 26

Victory and Victorious

With a good measure of confidence, Kyle entered his senior year of high school. After all the progress he had made his junior year, he knew he could handle any course work given to him, so he asked for, and was given, advanced placement classes in math, science, and social studies.

Robert kept drilling into Kyle's head, "Start each day in victory and end each day victorious". Kyle was taught to welcome each day as a proven winner, a victor, anticipating great things to happen and end each day knowing that he is victorious.

With Robert's encouragement, Kyle began to apply to universities that offered a major course of study that might lead to a lucrative career. Kyle had no idea how he would afford college, but his mother kept telling him not to worry about money and just to keep doing his best in high school. Kyle told his mom not to count on scholarship funds because they tend to be unpredictable according to his guidance councelor. Nevertheless, Avril was adamant regarding money for college in repeatedly saying to her son, "Don't worry about it".

Kyle truly enjoyed his classes during his senior year, engaging his teachers in spirited debates on topics germane to different subject areas. He particularly liked Ms. Maukas, his homeroom, and social studies teacher, who persuaded him to join various student organizations.

No matter how busy his school schedule would become Kyle would take a daily pilgrimage to the auditorium lobby where on the east wall was an enormous glass covered photo of the previous year's senior class. In that photo in the second row, the fifth student from the left was Denise. Kyle would stand in front of her in the photo, gaze at her, remember her voice and end by placing his fingers on her face. This everyday custom of Kyle's did not escape the notice of other students and faculty members who sometimes asked if the person he touched in the class photo had died. Kyle would just smile at the inquiring party and say only, "... she's very much alive."

Kyle never stopped trying to reach Denise, calling the university she told him that she would be attending. For security reasons, they would not provide any information on Denise's whereabouts, on or off campus. Kyle wrote to Denise in care of the university, but he never received a response from her written or by phone. This in no way deterred him continuing his efforts to find and communicate with Denise.

Kyle had framed the 5x7 inch photo of Denise and kept it on his night table, near his bed. Just before he laid his head on the pillow for sleep, he would talk to the photo ... to Denise. He would tell her of the things that happened that day and ask her opinion about decisions that he had to make. He always ended his night talks to her photo with the words, "Denise where ever you are, ... may flights of angels sing thee to thy rest."

His mother would often hear him talking to Denise through the wall between their bedrooms. Avril tried not to listen but could not help herself. Sometimes, while listening she would shed a tear, hearing the longing in Kyle's voice for a girl that he may never see again.

The September to June of Kyle's 12th grade year was replete with academic awards and moments for Kyle to bask in the glow of his achievements.

During the spring he was honored by two nationally known civic organizations, but Avril was unable to attend either function because of the demands of the two jobs she continued to work. Despite his so-so freshman year grades, Kyle rose in his class standings, earning all A's in every class since the second semester of his junior year.

Avril, so proud of her son, credited the appearance of "The Girl", Denise, in his life for these accomplishments. She could not figure out why or how this girl she had never met brought out the best in Kyle. Avril would not question providence, but she continued to thank God for Denise, hoping one day to thank her in person.

At Kyle's high school graduation ceremony on the football field, under a blazing sun, Avril sat alone in the bleachers under a large floppy hat. She beamed with pride as Kyle was introduced as the recipient of a number of senior awards and scholarships. With every monetary award, Avril thanked God. Avril did not recognize the names of any of the other seniors announced that day as she was never able to participate in Kyle's school activities. She watched her son offer congratulations to other students who were graduating and felt bad that she never met any of Kyle's classmates or teachers over the years.

Just before the awarding of diplomas, the superintendent of schools came to the podium to present a special scholarship from one of the state universities. He spoke of one student's dramatic rise in his school work and how unprecedented this young man's improvement had been. The award included two years of free tuition, with room, board, and books. At the end of this rather lengthy introduction, the superintendent announced the recipient as Kyle.

The entire senior class stood and applauded Kyle. Avril thought, "three short years ago, my son was virtually invisible in school, labeled a "marginalized" student by his guidance councelor. As Avril openly cried in the stands, she thought of the work Robert, his mentor had done with Kyle, the grace of God to overcome the deficiencies in her own life that held Kyle back ... and the mere presence of one person in Kyle's life.

God had ordained that Denise would change Kyle's life. She did and would continue to bless him for the rest of his life.

Chapter 26

Arvil's Time, a Time to Talk Again

With a scholarship in hand, Kyle began his collegiate years at the state university. He wasted no time in establishing himself as a high performing student as an Economics and Finance major. He achieved a 4.0 grade point average in both his freshman and sophomore years, grinding his way through the gut liberal arts courses that all university students must take.

Kyle's sophomore year at the university was marked by many positives. Despite his challenging major in finance, his grades were nothing less than outstanding. After the first semester, Kyle returned home for the holidays with Dean's List grades. His mother could not have been happier with his performance and the direction of his life.

As Avril struggled to maintain her two- job work schedule, she was not able to pick Kyle up at the university at the conclusion of the first semester. Fortunately, he was able to get a ride with one of his fraternity brothers who lived a town over.

Kyle had not seen his mother since September and was anxious to let her ask all the routine questions she showered him with every time they talked over the phone. As Kyle entered their apartment on that Friday evening, Avril was still not home from her second job, so he went about the first priority upon getting back in town ... calling people to see if they had seen Denise.

Kyle had not heard from Denise since a few weeks after her graduation day, 4 years, 5 months, and 13 days if anyone was counting ... and Kyle was. He would step up his "Denise research" in the week ahead as he was back in town, but he could not understand how she could have just dropped out of sight, or fathom how no one had heard from her. Preparing to make a call to the home of Denise's high school class president, Ken Metzer, he heard the apartment door open.

Kyle took a few steps in the direction of the door and caught the first look at his mother in three months. He looked at her and Avril said, "Now, don't say anything. I know it looks like I put on a few pounds".

Kyle's mother was slightly built with very thin legs, but for the first time, she had a bit of a belly. Kyle had to ask, "So mom did you discover Hungarian food, or are you just forgetting to put down the fork?"

"As a matter of fact, son of mine, I hardly have an appetite anymore and even when I do eat, I get filled up after a few mouthfuls," Avril explained.

Kyle flipped roles and played parent, "Mother don't you think it's time to get to a doctor and figure out what could be causing this?"

"I admit I am needing to pee every other minute, but that could be nothing more than being nervous or having a urinary tract infection," asserted Avril.

Kyle wanted to come down harder on his mother, "What have you got to be nervous about? Monday morning we're going to the walk-in clinic. Come to think of it, let's go to the clinic tomorrow morning."

Reasserting her parental status, "Kyle, you know I work a longer shift on Saturday. There is no need to miss work. I feel fine."

In fact, Avril was not feeling fine and hadn't in a while. Lately, she was feeling tired and having a hard time getting started in the morning. She was constipated almost daily and was experiencing stomach pain. All of this would be kept to herself. She would say no more to her son regarding her health ... at least for the time being.

She needed to have one of those long talks with her son real soon, maybe today. They only had each other in this world, but even though she did not want to burden him with any worries, the time had come to discuss the future with him.

On Christmas Eve Avril and Kyle headed to church to thank God for the greatest gift of all, the birth of our Lord and Savior, Christ Jesus. There was a great atmosphere across the congregation as one would expect on this evening. Following the service, Avril and Kyle made the rounds, saying hello to so many people Kyle had not seen in some time. The minister, the good Reverend Brookshire, approached Kyle and asked to talk with him for a few minutes.

Reverend Brookshire, an elderly man of 73, mentioned to Kyle that Avril had not looked herself in recent months and he had some concerns relative to her health. Kyle told him that he too noticed some changes in her appearance and that his mother had shared with him some symptoms she was experiencing. One of the problems, Kyle added, is that his mother has never complained about anything so he never knows if she is sick or feeling the least bit ill.

As he was returning to the university in the next few weeks after the holiday season, Kyle asked the minister to call him if he had the slightest inclination that his mother might be suffering in silence for any reason. Reverend Brookshire took a deep breath and said, "Your mother is extremely proud of you. We all love her and I promise we will take good care of her."

Avril asked Kyle to drive them home to their apartment. As his mother always insisted on driving everywhere, Kyle inquired, "Mom, don't you feel well?"

Avril turned to Kyle with some indignation and snapped, "You, my son, borrowed my car not too many years ago to drive "Miss Denise" home. Do you remember that foray of chivalry? So now on Christmas Eve, you can drive "Miss Avril", your mother, home so that I can see the Christmas decorations around town."

Kyle scooted around the passenger side of the car to open the door for his mother as every polite son should. When they were both seat belted in the car, Kyle drove to main and center streets where the many 100 year old homes were ornately decorated with traditional Christmas colors and symbols of the season.

After 20 minutes of driving through various neighborhoods and passing store fronts, Avril told Kyle they needed to talk. Kyle believing this to be a precursor for a serious lecture about his life and future, he asked his mother if this conversation might be put off until after the holidays.

Avril was steadfast, "Kyle, you are the best son any mother could have and I am so proud of all that you have accomplished, but there is no good time to talk about some things."

Kyle sensing that this might be something far more serious than his job prospects in the future, he suggested they go home for this talk.

"You need to hear this <u>now</u>," emphasized his mother.

"Keep your eyes on the road. I'll do the talking," instructed Avril.

"Let me begin with the most important thing I want to share with you. Do you remember when we had those discussions about love and I told you to find your ways to love? Well, there is more to love than just taking the best of your God-given gifts and using them to show others you care," began Avril.

"Son, the principle you need to understand is that "Love in not an emotion … It's an act of will.""

Choking up, his mother explained, "When you were born I loved you. I always will. Those are feelings deep in a mother's heart, but feeling is not enough. Love requires that you act, do the things necessary to validate the meaning of the feeling. Kyle, my love for you placed me in a position that I was forced to act when you were born. My first act of will was to bring you up by myself and that meant putting you first in all facets of my life. That was an easy decision for me. You are that precious to me. However, that act of will had some tough parts to it. I knew that without any education beyond high school,

I would have to take a job or more than one job so that we could live as normal a life as possible."

Kyle drove along the snow covered streets, his eyes on the roads, listening to every word, but had to comment, "Mom don't you think I appreciate all you have done for me?"

"Son you need just to listen," continued his mother, "... you know that I have saved every dime and dollar, week after week. There was a reason that we didn't go hardly anywhere or why we never had a home of our own, or why I drive a used car."

Kyle interrupted again, "Mom you don't have to explain anything to me."

"I do," Avril asserted, "Just listen, please. By the grace of God, you had your first two years of college almost totally paid for by scholarship. When we get home, I will be handing you a passbook for a savings account. In it, there is more than enough to pay for your last two years in college."

Kyle had to ask, "Why are you telling me all this tonight? What's going on? It's Christmas Eve."

Avril quietly replied, "Son, I have ovarian cancer."

Kyle immediately pulled the car over to the side of the road and began to cry as his mother wrapped her arms around him.

"There was no right time or place to tell you, but you needed to know," explained Avril.

Avril went on to explain that this form of cancer moves rapidly and when she finally went to see a doctor, the cancer was pretty far along. Candidly, she told her son of the symptoms she had been experiencing for the past five months and what she was told she could expect moving forward.

Kyle realizing that he needed to enact his own "act of will", declared, "Mom I'll take off a semester to be with you. We can see this through together."

"You will do no such thing, not on my watch my son. I don't love you the way I love you and always will love you and now let you drop out of college. I must do this my way and all you owe me is to comply with my wishes," explained Avril.

"Son, listen to me. I have had all the treatments I am going have ... made all the preparations with my doctors, insurance company ...with my employers ... with the church. I have church members ready to help in a lot of ways. Please do what I ask."

Kyle cried for some time, trying to come to grips with what just had been told to him. It was a long night for both of them. Kyle would not leave his mother's side. He suggested a hundred things he wanted to do for her and asked about what the doctors had in mind moving forward.

Avril exhausted and in some pain told Kyle that he could accompany her to the hospital for a treatment she was having the following week. She told Kyle that he could ask the doctor any questions he would like, but wanted Kyle to know that the verdict, the outcome, of this disease was certain and soon.

Together, they would enjoy this final Christmas. There would be no mention of Avril's cancer on Christmas day.

There was a helpless emptiness inside Kyle in the weeks to come. The doctor explained to Kyle that his mother's cancer did not leave her much time. Kyle did as she mother told him and returned to the university where they talked on the phone often times every day. Avril was admitted to the hospital, then to Hospice six weeks after the start of the semester.

Kyle took a few dollars from his college savings account for bus fare home as soon as he was called that his mother was in Hospice care.

He arrived on Wednesday afternoon as Reverend Brookshire was at Avril's bedside. She was hardly able to speak or open her eyes and had a slight yellow color to her skin.

Kyle sunk to his knees and taking her hand told her of his endless love for her. Tears streamed down his face as he tried to pry every word of thanks from his heart. With suddenness, she was gone. The minister prayed over her, and despite his words of sympathy, Kyle was alone, a type of isolation that he had never experienced before.

After some hours, Kyle left his mother's bedside and walked out into the wintery gardens of the Hospice facility. He walked along the brick and asphalt sidewalks that wove through the grounds and came to a bench near a small man-made pond. There, he was hit by a new wave of sadness and looking skyward, screamed, "DENISE HELP ME ... HELP ME PLEASE". In his time of need after prayers had been made, Kyle sought out the only person who could comfort him.

Chapter 27

Carrying on Without Mom

The death of his mother near the end of his sophomore year of college ostensibly changed how he looked at his life, more immediately how he viewed his college education. Gone were the encouraging words of his mother who displayed such enjoyment that her son was a "college man". Denied her own opportunity for a collegiate experience, Avril surely lived vicariously through Kyle's late surge of high school academic success and his every little victory in college.

During his freshman and sophomore years in college, Kyle would often ask his mother to stop asking so many questions about his every activity over the phone. Avril would ask Kyle if he met a pretty girl. ... Did he attend athletic events or see anything interesting on campus? Despite the annoyance of answering the same kinds of questions from his mother in every phone call, Kyle understood his mother's sincere desire to in some way share his college experience.

When Avril died the biggest piece of his life went away. Gone was the safety net of family that provided a confidence that he wasn't ever totally alone. At college, away from home, he could always pick up the phone and call his mother, should he feel lonely, or just need to hear a voice that expressed love by just the sound. It was only now that Kyle recognized how he took his mother's place in his life for granted. No other person in his life except the pristine Denise and his mother could fortify his heart. Now both were absent from his heart, mom by death and Denise by disappearance. He missed them both so much, for such different reasons, and if he allowed himself to think of them, he welled up in tears at any time, in any place.

Kyle continued his vigil in college to find Denise. He called her old number, knowing that it was a disconnected cell number. He called the cellphone provider and tried every search engine that he could find on line. Kyle even tried to locate Frank. Just maybe through him, he would locate Denise, but that effort similarly came up void. He drove to the house where Denise used to live, knowing her parents had moved away after she graduated from high school. He questioned the current residents as to the former occupants' current status, but they claimed ignorance.

Kyle never stopped adoring Denise, revering her in every way. She was no fantasy. She was all together real in every way and Kyle committed himself to never stop looking for her, no matter where it might lead. With his mother's death, there was finality, closure. There was nothing more to be done, but to keep her memory and all that Avril had taught him alive in how he conducted his life, but Denise was out there, somewhere, waiting to be found.

At the outset of his junior year at the university, Kyle adjusted his life without his mother. In order not to feel sorry for himself or do that "woe is me" thing people tend to do after someone passes on in their lives, Kyle threw himself, more than ever, into his courses, and activities.

Kyle's plan was to leave little time to lament or grieve his mother's death. He remembered the words of the eulogy he wrote and spoke at his mother's funeral. As he was the only family Avril had, the eulogy was largely a self-designed pledge to his mother for his future. He called on God to guide his path in the days ahead, citing, Jeremiah 29:11, "For I know the plans and thoughts that I have for you,' says the LORD, 'plans for peace and well-being and not for disaster, to give you a future and a hope."

Kyle trusted in God, now more than ever. He prayed that his life would be filled with victories that served others ... and each night, Kyle prayed that God would bring Denise back into his life.

With the galvanizing resolve made to God following the death of his mom, Kyle increased his level of commitment as an Economics and Finance major. He selected some of the most demanding professors in the department, knowing full well that a greater work load would follow. Additionally, Kyle's fraternity that he successfully pledged in the spring of his sophomore year at his mother's behest had elected him an officer for this year, "Executive Treasurer", the first office of any kind he had held in his life. He thought how much that would have made her smile if she was alive.

Chapter 29

Some Things Don't Change

Kyle didn't date in high school. Although he improved as a student his social interaction with others, especially girls was negligible ... other than the many hours of telephone friendship with Denise. The time talking with Denise built his confidence somewhat, but no girl could come close to equaling what Denise meant to Kyle. Even after Denise graduated he felt no real desire to find a girl to date or befriend.

Try as he might, *through eyes that were only for Denise,* to find a girl to ask to his senior prom, the bar was just set too high. Avril's words haunted him, "There is only one", and to Kyle, "The One" was Denise! Kyle rarely talked about Denise to his mother during his senior year in high school as their telephone time stopped with Denise away at college.

Once in college himself, Kyle witnessed a whole new definition to the word "freedom". Rules, if there were any, for drinking, dating activity, language and basic comportment between students were so casual that Kyle could hardly find a place to fit in. It wasn't like high school, it was worse. He kept to himself throughout most of his freshman and sophomore years and it was only at the urging of his mother that he decided to join a fraternity. It was an organization of mostly finance and math majors, and although there were some rather wild persons in the frat, it was nowhere near the craziness of other fraternities on campus.

Throughout his years in college, Kyle kept the photo of Denise that she gave him for Christmas years ago, affixed to the wall near his bed at pillow level. Denise was the last thing he saw before the lights were turned out and the first thing he saw every morning when he awoke. Kyle treated the photo like gold, keeping it in a double covered see-thru sheet protector.

During the first two years of college life, Kyle met many students, worked in groups in a number of classes and became comfortable with many types of social circumstances but one. Although he did attend social functions, college events with others, he still chose not to ask anyone out on a date.

Chapter 29

Insensitivity

At the outset of the fall semester his junior year Kyle's fraternity planned their annual formal gala, a fund raising function, to welcome back alumni of the fraternity. All the current members of the organization were required to attend with a guest. As an officer, Kyle was in a difficult position. He had to attend but did not want to go through the aggravation of finding, asking, and escorting a date to the function.

At the executive board meeting of the fraternity, some three weeks before the gala, Kyle requested of the board for a waiver of the organizational mandate to be permitted to come alone to the formal.

After rigorous debate, the senior members of the board decided to meet privately in closed session and discuss Kyle's request. After 20 minutes the senior board emerged and told Kyle that he would be permitted to come alone with the caveat that he fully participates in the opening promenade, a walk-in, of fraternity officers and their dates.

Kyle was pleased, yet stunned by their ruling, anticipating that they might find a date for him, but he was about to be more shocked by what they had in mind for him.

The evening of the gala, a beautiful October Saturday, underclass members of the fraternity stood by the entrance of Vanderkelen Hall to welcome the alumni and upper-class members of the fraternity. Kyle walked in without talking to anyone, alone as usual, and entered the magnificently decorated hall.

After some preliminary toasts, all the guests took their seats and the officers of the fraternity assembled at the back of the hall for the traditional promenade.

As Kyle was without a female companion, he was placed at the back of the line. He waited patiently for each of the tuxedoed honored guests and officers to be introduced by title, name, along with *their respective date's name* to the live music of the Matrovan Orchestra.

When it was Kyle's turn to walk through the receiving line of the gauntlet formed by standing fraternity members, the master of ceremonies, spoke with an exceptionally slower pace, "Fellow brothers and sisters, honored guests, ladies and gentlemen all, we are proud to introduce our Executive Treasurer, Kyle and his Lady Fair, DENISE. With that pronouncement of "her name" an actual six foot photo poster of "Denise" was raised from the first table facing the opulent entrance.

An astonished Kyle did not laugh, although most others did. His eyes filled with tears as he stood motionless staring at a replica of the photo of Denise that was so discretely displayed near his pillow by his bed.

He knew in an instant that the fraternity had removed the photo from his wall and had it blown up for the poster that now brought hoots, laughter, and applause from the assembled masses.

A knot was forged in Kyle's throat and his breathing was a pattern of quick breaths as he tried to compose his emotions. Kyle was not really angry. Kyle was overwhelmed by this public disclosure of his love for Denise. He had rarely talked about her with anyone other than with his mother and Robert. As if his entire life had been torn open for all to see, he was confronted by his own passion, never so unleashed as in this moment of embarrassment and downright insensitivity by his supposed brothers and sisters in the fraternity.

Kyle walked the center aisle as did those who preceded him to his seat on the dais at the front of the room. He never smiled or acknowledged a single person along the walk. Kyle had to force himself to keep his chin up as the emotion of this calamity yanked at his faltering composure.

An elegant dinner was served by white jacketed waiters, as Kyle coyly moved the served food about the plate, trying only to be polite and visibly unobtrusive as his every thought was of Denise. If there was ever doubt or a misrepresentation of his feelings before, there was no longer. He knew and was certain how to define his feelings for Denise. Where ever she really was in this world, if she was even alive, Denise was now Kyle's heart. This callous act had ripped down the façade of self-denial about his true feelings for this girl.

Denise now became, forever more to be so recognized by Kyle as THE ONE ... and as Kyle was so inculcated by his mother those many years ago, ... THERE IS ONLY ONE. It had been a truth within his heart for four years, now it stood brilliantly as a fact in his body, mind, soul, and heart.

Kyle left the gala by a side door as soon as the dancing began in earnest. He did not stop to bid adieu or provide an opportunity for anyone to explain or further exacerbate what had occurred. He openly sobbed as he walked back to his room, more so than when he first learned of his mother's death. He talked out loud to Denise, something he would do many times in the years to come. He asked God to bring his words to the ear and heart of Denise.

Upon entering his room, he turned the light on to discover that the small graduation photo of Denise was right where he left it, sitting by his bedside, covered in plastic, just above his pillow. Fully clothed he lay on his bed and placed his lips on the photo of this one in a lifetime girl.

Kyle wondered ... If Denise ever knew how he felt about her, what would she say? Sometime that evening Kyle would drift off to sleep with thoughts of only Denise.

Chapter 30

The Three Diamond Ring

As he began mentally preparing for each of the very demanding classes, all in his major, he noted a course that he thought might lead to a possible career in the area of financial planning, "Personal Economics and Financial Planning". However, he saw that the professor was to be Dr. Melvin G. Bunker, better known as the "professor vagus" (the *unpredictable professor* in Latin). In the instruction of finance and economics, Dr. Bunker disdained rote learning, couldn't stand traditional, "direct from-the-text", students. He encouraged original conceptualization and insisted upon "out-of-the-box" thinking. When you had Dr. Bunker for a class, you never knew what he was going to do, or ask you to do.

Kyle had previously taken Dr. Bunker for "Econometrics". During that semester, Dr. Bunker's demands for creativity in the use and interpretation of statistics in every paper and project were ever present. Kyle met with Dr. Bunker more than a few times during that semester as Kyle initially was having a difficult time with the material. So Bunker and Kyle knew each other and generally got along very well.

One the first day of class of "Personal Economics and Financial Planning" Dr. Bunker explained an end-of-course project that all students would need to complete, entitled "Invest in Your Future". He detailed a procedure where each student would design a plan for investment in a significant life event.

Bunker's assignment was right in keeping with his nickname, unpredictable, as it seemed that this project was all too simple, more in line with a high school or community college project.

When he had finished his description of the assignment and handed out the outline for the "Personal Finance Project", one student raised her hand and asked, "Dr. Bunker are you suggesting that we may choose to do something as basic as financing a car or paying for graduate school?"

Bunker rubbed his chin and expanded his thinking, "Ladies and gentlemen, I am of the opinion that few young people today, truly plan for the future or know how. It is not strictly a matter of money or banking, but purpose and vision."

"LOOK INTO YOUR FUTURE," Bunker barked. "Come up with an idea that has viability and meaning in, and for your future. I will expect an abstract of your project in two weeks as per the handout".

Kyle left class that day with no hint of an idea for the project. He walked over to the Student Union building where he held a part time job, cleaning meeting rooms a few hours a week. Changing into his uniform overalls he racked his brain for an idea, but nothing of meaning came to him.

As he dusted and picked up loose paper on the floor of the room he was cleaning, his thoughts departed Dr. Bunker's task ... and found Denise, always the best landing place for his heart and mind. He wished he knew where she was, longing to hear the soft velvetiness of her voice once more.

After he cleaned up and changed again, he headed for his next class and saw a long banner hanging over the library entrance with the printing, "plan for your future". Cynically, he thought, "what future". Looking to the future seemed a lot easier a year or two ago, now with mom gone, the future was just a lonely place.

That evening, with his heart feeling too down to get anything meaningful done with study, he decided to call Robert, his high school mentor. He hadn't talked to Robert since just after the funeral, and he needed to clear his head, so he called. At the least, Robert was always good for a laugh.

Robert picked up on the first ring and opened with ... "so you heard from Denise huh?"

Kyle's heart jumped through his chest, "What? What do you mean? Do you know where she is?"

Robert immediately apologized, "Hey, look, I am sorry, for some reason I thought you were calling me because you heard from her. Sorry, didn't mean to make you crazy."

With order restored, Kyle and Robert caught up on things with Kyle getting around to explaining the personal finance assignment of Dr. Bunker. As always Robert was easily focused on whatever topic they discussed. Robert suggested financial planning ideas that had to do with purchasing a home, furniture, a special event, having children, and planning for old age.

Kyle was limping in this conversation because so much of what Robert mentioned had to do with marriage and sharing things with others in life. Kyle just could not get his arms around the institution of marriage, feeling so alone these days.

Robert sensing Kyle's mood offered up an idea. "Listen", Robert began, "... I have no doubt that you will meet someone, fall in love, like everyone does, sooner or later, and get around to marriage."

Kyle was bothered by Robert's words. "You know, all this stuff about love and marriage, maybe it wasn't meant for me", announced Kyle. He continued, "The whole process of two people arranging to legally join and then mix in who loves who and to what extent, and with what limitations. It all seems so confusing to me".

Robert always knew there were a ton of emotions tucked up inside Kyle, most of them sitting by a door that led only to this girl, Denise. Robert was aware that any discussion of Denise would result in a very emotional response. A perceptive mentor and friend, Robert recognized that Kyle had never ever really acknowledged that he *loved* Denise.

Kyle had done so many things to love Denise in his own

way by listening, the giving of humble little gifts and most of all honoring her with his heart, but Kyle never actually said the words, "I love you" to her, or admitted it to Robert or his mother. Clearly, those three words had the most important meaning to Kyle. They could not leave his lips with any full meaning unless they were heard by Denise, and he longed to hear them from Denise if that would have ever been possible.

Robert became more direct in his words, "Kyle, it is time you understood something about two people who love each other. A meaningful relationship begins by taking the essence, the best of each person, entwining both, making them far greater together than anything they are as individuals or alone.

Kyle had hoped the conversation with Robert would lead to an idea for Dr. Bunker's course. Instead, it just turned into a discussion about love and marriage.

With a need to back away from the latter topic, Kyle asked, "Robert got any ideas for the personal finance project?"

Robert sighed into his phone, figuring his fortuitous, mini-lecture on marriage would be meaningful to his mentee and said, "Kyle, you have a great heart and you were not meant to be alone. Why don't you come up with a personal finance project that includes a little basic math, like 1 + 1 = *Big* **1**."

Kyle wondered if Robert had lost his mind or was just busting 'em off" on Kyle with that silly equation.

With that, Robert wished him well and said good night.

Kyle looked into his phone, shook his head laughing and repeated, "1 + 1 = *Big* **1**, what did that mean?"

Chapter 31

Project of Passion

At the next class meeting of "Personal Economics and Financial Planning", most students had questions about the selection of a project. Kyle was glad it wasn't just him. Dr. Bunker seemed to be enjoying the discomfort of his students and took most of the class time to answer each student's query. Kyle listened intently to the other students and Dr. Bunker's comments as he scribbled Robert's big contribution of a few nights before, "1 + 1 = *Big* **1**".

Kyle looking for some inspiration or just some sanity in this task wrote "*invest in your future*, 1+1=**1**" on the cover of his notebook. He drew circles around each number and remembered when he would write "D's" around numbers in math class in high school thinking about Denise.

Now, almost instinctively, he wrote her former phone number and made a "D" out of each digit. Somehow just thinking of her made everything better.

As he exited class, Dr. Bunker called out, "Kyle, you have an investment in your future in mind? I didn't hear a single question from you today."

Kyle still lost in his thoughts of Denise, answered with an uncharacteristic *smart ass* comment, "Dr. Bunker we all know that an investment, if effective, results in a substantive outcome."

Dr. Bunker was taken aback by his usually reserved student, and kept up the repartee, "So then Kyle, my boy, what is your substantive outcome?"

Kyle, with spontaneity and candor, "I find THE girl."

A naughty little smile came upon Bunker's face as he ended the witty banter with, "Kyle I shall anxiously look forward to reading your abstract next week."

Leaving the room, an idea, something he had never even contemplated doing in his life, was to be his "investment" ... in <u>his</u> future. He would have to convince Dr. Bunker of the worthiness of this effort. He knew he would be sound in his design principles and what's more, his heart would be deeply behind it. The question was would Dr. Bunker approve it?

Chapter 32

Denise Devotion

Friday afternoon brought the buzz of the weekend's football game with all its parties and rallies, but Kyle was focused on writing an abstract for the "Investment in the Future" project. Seated in his self-appointed "study closet" in Pendleton Hall, the place on campus where he could always go to concentrate without distractions, Kyle worked on the plan.

He did not have a girl in his life, but he did have the vision of Denise and the belief that she was somewhere out there if only he could find her. In the end, it was a course project and he had to approach it as such. The topic box on the top of the abstract read:

Project:

Investment in an Engagement Ring

Purpose:

To be prepared for the perfect moment with the perfect girl, object matrimony.

Following Dr. Bunker's next class meeting, he collected everyone's abstract, at least those who completed the assignment. Kyle was anxious to get to his study of that night with an Accounting II test scheduled for the coming Monday.

Getting up to leave, Dr. Bunker called out to Kyle to remain after class. Not wishing to get involved in a long protracted conversation about his project, Kyle went over and stood next to Dr. Bunker's desk at the front of the room.

Bunker sifted through the abstracts on his desk looking for Kyle's project. Having located it, Bunker sat reading it for a moment, making him wait and then looked at Kyle with this professorial smugness some twisted inner humor, chided, "Kyle, do you really feel that I should approve such a jejune project? Are you actually going to stand there and tell me that you plan to purchase an engagement ring on time with no apparent object for the exercise ... a specific girl?"

Kyle was more than surprised at Bunker's attitude and answered back, "YES, I most certainly do expect you to approve it."

"Well Kyle, convince me! Make an argument."

Now, thoroughly in attack mode, Kyle harnessed his passion and cut loose with a bit of rhetorical reasoning that reflected the seasoned wisdom of his heart.

"Dr. Bunker," Kyle railed in opening fire, "I think you would concur that if a man is not prepared for his chance, his chance will only make him look foolish."

Additionally, I believe you would agree that asking someone to share your life in matrimony is not strictly a matter of love and good intentions, but a legally binding contract with specific fiduciary responsibilities and far reaching consequences."

Kyle was on the proverbial roll and wasn't sure what was coming out of his mouth next, "Let me further speculate that marriage works when we adhere to the formula, 1+1=Big 1."

Dr. Bunker, confused at this numerical tidbit, "Kyle slow down and explain that hunk of irreverent mathematics to me."

Kyle impulsively decided to explain his plan for the ring. "Dr. Bunker, each of us brings to a relationship an assortment of strengths and weaknesses, but the best of each of us is in how we demonstrate, express, our love to another person in deed, not necessarily in words. Therefore, we add the gift of individually styled love-giving from each person to the other. Then with synergistic harmony, they are greater than they could ever be as individuals."

Kyle summarized, "To wit, it is my plan to purchase as an investment in my future, an engagement ring with two average sized diamonds, symbolizing the two graced individuals preparing to be joined in marriage with a central single larger diamond, denoting their joining, becoming more than they ever dreamed they could be as individuals."

Bunker sat mesmerized, listening to Kyle espouse the reason for the most unique personal finance project he had ever heard. The professor stared at Kyle above the edges of his glasses and said, "Kyle, are you sure you don't have a girl in mind?"

Kyle smiled widely, "Dr. Bunker, do you like the name Denise?"

With that ... Dr. Bunker heartedly chuckled, picked up his pen and wrote "APPROVED" with his initials.

With the not so surprising approval of the abstract from the "professor vagus", Kyle approached the project with childlike joy.

As Saturday morning rolled around, the parking lots about campus were filled with students, alumni and tailgaters anticipating the day's rivalry football game. Kyle's plan for the day was very different. He borrowed a car from one of his fraternity brothers and drove through the crowded streets to the modest little strip mall in the middle of town, where Belton's Jewelers was located.

As he parked the borrowed car he could hear the sound of drums from campus and the crackle of the cheering crowd. On a piece of notebook paper, Kyle had sketched a rendering of what the three diamond ring would look like. Like most jewelry stores Belton's surely would have hundreds of engagement and wedding rings, and he knew the chances of finding the exact ring of his design were not favorable. However, the biggest factor in bringing this vision to reality was the cost of the ring and if he could arrange credit.

Although he had a bank account that his mother had left him, it was started by his mother many years ago for the sole purpose of paying for his college education, not to purchase engagement rings for a school project. After Avril had died, that bank account was his financial lifeline to complete college before initiating a career.

Entering the store a young sales lady was standing behind the main counter and asked if she could help him find something. Kyle took the drawing he made of the ring, then slowly and with meticulous consideration to detail, began to explain his purpose, the project itself and his plan. The sales girl listened to Kyle's general explanation and immediately realized she was not the best person to handle this customer. Excusing herself, she walked over to an elderly gentleman and said a few words to him.

The gentleman came over to Kyle and introducing himself as Barry Belton, the owner of the store. "How can I help you," Mr. Belton asked?

With the clearest explanation he could muster, Kyle detailed the situation, including the part that he had no money and was not regularly employed. Mr. Belton found some humor in this situation but was also sympathetic to this college student.

As the store was devoid of customers on this Saturday morning, Belton suggested that they first try to find a ring that met Kyle's specifications, three diamonds with a large diamond in the middle. The ring display case was filled with tray after tray of engagement and wedding rings, some with giant diamond settings, others with clusters of little diamond chips. After a solid hour of looking at every ring in every tray, Mr. Belton inquired, "Is it that important that the ring looks like the one you described?"

Kyle considered the question. In an instant, he reflected back on the conversation with Robert, his mother's teachings on love and most importantly, Denise. His response, "Mr. Belton, yes, it is that important."

Mr. Belton told Kyle that he could make a setting for him that would look like his sketch, but it would be very expensive.

With frustration edging into Kyle's heart, Mr. Belton recommended a different approach.

Asking Kyle to come into his office area at the back of the store, they sat down across from each other at a desk that was cluttered with stacks of paper. Mr. Belton explained that he was short staffed since his older daughter got married and moved away.

Hence, he offered Kyle a proposition. If Kyle would agree

to work in his store three nights a week and on Saturdays, Mr. Belton would create a ring just like the rendering in his sketch. Kyle not fully believing this offer, "Mr. Belton, are you proposing to construct a three diamond ring for me and my only obligation is to work for you?"

Belton clarified his offer, "Kyle, I just met you; however, something tells me you are one unique young man. I'm a rather good judge of character."

So, as a trained jeweler of some skill, yes I will create a ring from your drawing with two medium sized diamonds flanking a bigger diamond in the middle with the understanding that you work here in my store doing any and all tasks I assign to you with no other compensation ... meaning I will not give you a pay check. However, if you fail to work the required days, our agreement will be cancelled and ... you won't get the ring,"

Kyle almost forgot the biggest reason for doing this ... Dr. Bunker's project. "Mr. Belton since this is a college project, could we draw up some kind of statement of understanding or a contract that I can give to my college professor to prove I am doing this?"

Mr. Belton agreed to draft a contract that both would sign as the owner concluded this impromptu negotiation with, "... by the way, you start today."

For almost five months Kyle worked diligently in the evening store hours at Belton's, helping the owner organize his paperwork, pay invoices, keeping Belton's desk clean and do general accounting tasks. Mr. Belton never asked Kyle to serve customers as a sales clerk, but Kyle would often wrap packages and run customer credit cards.

Without his mother to go home to for the holidays, Kyle stayed on campus at his fraternity house, offering to work more hours and additional days. Kyle enjoyed working at the store and Belton found Kyle's effort and enthusiasm a very special addition to his business.

As the beginning of the spring semester was about to commence in January, Kyle was faced with a new schedule of classes with one required course in his major, "Tax Accounting" that met in the evenings. This would mean that he would be hard pressed to continue his current arrangement with Mr. Belton.

With a heavy heart and his new spring semester schedule in his hand, Kyle arrived early on Monday needing to talk with Mr. Belton. Kyle walked to be back of the store where Mr. Belton was seated at his desk that was clean and organized a far cry from the messy desk that Kyle recalled from their first meeting.

Kyle explained that despite his best efforts to keep his calendar at the university clear so there would never be a conflict in his work schedule as they had agreed, he now had a course that he must take, preventing him from maintaining the same schedule.

Mr. Belton looked at his young employee, "Kyle, I am so disappointed by this development. You know this may abrogate our agreement. Are you prepared to give up on the ring idea?"

Kyle's face turned to one of sadness but understood that a contract was written and they both agreed. With that, Mr. Belton asked Kyle to wait there at the desk for a minute. As Kyle waited he thought of a compromise he might put forth that would that prompt Mr. Belton to give him different work hours. He enjoyed working at the store but doing everything possible to get that ring had come to be so important to him.

As Mr. Belton sat down at his desk, Kyle started to express how much he liked working at the store and how much he appreciated the opportunity that Mr. Belton had given him.

With Mr. Belton breaking out in a wide grin, "Kyle, would you do me one last favor and remain silent for a while?"

Kyle complied as Mr. Belton took a small light grey box from inside his sports coat and handed to him. Kyle looked at his his employer and spoke, "You didn't have to do this."

"Open it ... now," Belton commanded.

Slowly, with long-seeded anticipation, Kyle opened the box. Inside he saw the fullest manifestation of the three diamond ring that began with his conversation with Robert, his mentor. Two diamonds, much larger than what he had envisioned flanked the largest diamond in the middle. The ring was more beautiful than he ever imagined it could be.

"You more than earned it Kyle. You now have an engagement ring. Now, I have a question I have wanted to ask since you first came into my shop. Who is this ring for?"

Kyle looked at his boss who had treated him so kindly these past months, "Mr. Belton, I don't have a girlfriend. I have never asked a girl to marry me."

Mr. Belton looked at Kyle with the perception to know that something was not being said, "Kyle no one goes through all that you have, the many hours of late night work, no pay, no compensation at all, other than the promise of a ring unless you have a greater purpose."

Kyle feeling the need to provide some explanation, "Mr. Belton there is a someone ... The Girl ... but she doesn't know it. I've never dated her or expressed how I feel to her, but she never leaves my heart. I don't know where she is, or even if she is alive. The only thing I know for sure is her name ... Denise."

Mr. Belton and Kyle talked for a while about things other than the ring. Kyle mentioned that he would like to continue working at the store, but Belton told him that as much as he would like Kyle to stay he couldn't afford to take on another employee, now that the holiday season had concluded.

Kyle held the ring box as tightly in his hand as he could, hugged Mr. Belton, thanked him for his kindness and the two parted ways at the front door of the store.

Kyle, ring in hand, strolled the long walk back to campus. He needed to think. He wondered if he would ever give the ring to anyone. Then catching the absurdity of his silly question knew that if he did not find and give this ring to Denise, it would sit in a drawer for the rest of his life.

Kyle would seek out Dr. Bunker in the next few weeks and show him the fruits of his labors and maybe that would be the last Kyle would see of the ring as he would put it away for safe keeping.

Chapter 34

Senior Sprint to the Future

The second semester of Kyle's junior year at the university was packed with challenging course work, community service, and campus activities, but never did a day pass that he didn't take a look at the 3-diamond ring and think of Denise. No matter the place or the difficulty of the task he faced, it was always made better by thoughts of her.

In her absence, Denise had become Kyle's source of motivation, inspiration, and in many ways his heartbeat. He knew there was the possibility that he might never see her again. Maybe she was lost to him forever years ago. All he could do was listen to his heart as his mother had taught him long ago.

Due to his high grades and a few timely letters of recommendations from his professors, Kyle earned an internship at a prestigious bank in Philadelphia for the summer prior to his senior year. The work was laborious and the hours were long, but he loved working with professional financial analysts who taught him many nuances about the industry. He learned that fact finding was a very sophisticated aspect of personal finance, especially when it came to helping families locate lost or misplaced assets and the disposition of next of kin. When he saw the techniques, software, and processes for finding someone, he thought, at long last, he may have found a way to locate ... DENISE.

In the evening at the apartment that he shared with three other interns, he would scour the internet in hopes of finding her, but alas every effort came up a dead end. The staff and other interns of the firm considered Kyle to be charming and affable, but he still kept to himself and rarely dated. Kyle carried himself as a professional and never postured for future employment or to impress anyone. Kyle had learned to believe in the dignity of work and that meant every minute in the service of a customer, or his firm was precious, requiring his best effort.

Kyle's internship ended a few days before the beginning of his fourth and final year of undergraduate studies at the university. He was one of the top students entering his senior year and there was no slowing down the academic ascent of Kyle.

The year flew by with few free moments to search for Denise, but each day when he returned to his room in the fraternity house there was the 5x7 photo of Denise by his bed, the one she had given to him. Each day he would hold it in his hand and remember that Denise touched it and that made it ever so special to him. There was no hand-written message on the back side of the photo from Denise, but every now and then, Kyle would imagine what she might have written to him.

Kyle would talk to the photo of Denise, telling her all the stored up things in his heart. He extolled his admiration for her in endless ways, praised her beauty in every detail, but always refrained from saying the words that were meant for only her ears ... "I love you". He could not say them to a picture. Kyle hadn't said those words since the final moments of his mother's life.

Sometimes when he talked to the picture, he would place his finger on the glass of the frame that housed the photo and slowly outlined her lips ... just as he did to her so long ago. Kyle was often filled with tears staring at the image of her in the photo.

As awards and pieces of recognition that Kyle earned came

along, he would enter his room and yell out, "Denise, guess what happened to me today"?

With each little talk Kyle had with the photo of Denise, it always ended with a pleading that completely spilled out from his heart, "Denise, please come to me. Please let me find you."

The first week in May for most universities culminates in commencement day, a time for each graduate to come forward and receive their earned degree in front of family, and their fellow classmates. For Kyle, Commencement Day would be one of mixed emotions. He would graduate with Summa Cum Laude status, honored with the annual Bernard O'Brien Prize for character and leadership, and receive the Gaetano Goldstein Medal as the top ranked senior in his major of finance.

Kyle was given five tickets for the commencement ceremony that are intended to be given to family and friends. Sadly, Kyle's mother who saved every dime and dollar to make college possible for him would not be there. Robert, his mentor, had only recently taken a position in Phoenix, Arizona and would not be able to attend. Under his graduation cap, Kyle wrote the following, "Mom, you gave me life; you gave me a college education. Robert, you gave me friendship. Thank you for making this day possible."

Kyle gave four of his five tickets to senior members of his fraternity. The day before commencement, Kyle walked down to Angelone Field House, the location of the ceremony. The 10,000 seat arena was traditionally decorated with banners, flags and a large stage area at the south end of the field house. Just outside the north entrance doors was the "Will-Call" box office. This was the place where tickets could be left for special guests and late-arriving family members of graduating seniors. Kyle approached one of the attendants working there and asked to leave a ticket for someone for commencement. Kyle reached into his jacket and pulled out an unsealed envelope. Written on the envelope was his name, the seat number 1172, and in capital letters, DENISE. Before sealing the envelope, he withdrew a note from inside that was folded around the ticket that read:

Dear Denise,
Thank you for sharing this day with me.
You have been with me each day in college.
You will be with me forever.

Kyle licked the seal on the flap on the envelope and handed to the attendant. Where ever in the world Denise would be the following morning, Kyle would believe that she was there. As he was introduced, walked the stage to receive his degree, he would glance over the gathered throng to seek her face. It was a fitting gesture to "the girl" who had impacted him so much.

Chapter 34

A Final Look Back Before Leaping Forward

As Kyle's grades improved by leaps and bounds in the last two years of high school he altered his attitude regarding college. With his first trip to the honor roll, Kyle looked at himself in a whole different light. He began to realize that college was something he really could do. Once more, attending a university was something he wanted to do and he discussed it with Robert.

In the hours of guidance and encouragement that Robert imparted to his young mentee was the need to have a clear purpose for going to a specific college. Most high school students have their eye on college as a post-high school landing place, but few seem to have a specific reason for going. With the thousands of dollars required to matriculate to a college that is usually paid through a series of heavy interest loans, whether one graduates or not, it is critical to have a reason to go there because one way or another, you are going to pay for it.

Robert asserted that possessing a personal focused mission for going to college would provide extra motivation when one is confronted with the challenges of college life. Given that college is not a required part of life, despite parental pressure to the contrary, most college students will admit to themselves, sooner or later, "I don't have to do this".

Kyle chose his university well, and he was accepted to

both his first two choices because his record of achievement continued to improve to high levels of achievement. By his senior year, he knew he wanted to pursue a career in finance and banking.

Now the time had come to take his degree and all that he had learned in college and begin a career. In February Kyle had sent out his resume to a number of companies and firms in the highly competitive world of finance. Kyle didn't have to wait long to be contacted by a few firms to come in for an interview.

By early April Kyle had his second interview with Saty Financial, LLC of Philadelphia, one of the most influential private wealth investment firms in the country. On April 22nd Kyle accepted the position of Associate of Analytics and a career that he had envisioned since his senior year in high school would begin immediately after commencement.

As one could imagine, Kyle was teeming with excitement over his first job in finance. He wanted to share the moment as anyone would. Kyle's first and only thought was that he wished he could call Denise and tell her all about what just happened. Kyle had gotten used to being alone in his life. He never felt sorry for himself, but came close at this moment. As he had at other times ... in other places ... in different circumstances since Denise disappeared, he created his own little reality.

Standing outside of the Saty Financial office building on Rittenhouse Square he surveyed his new surroundings. Seeing a nearby park, he walked to its bricked sidewalk that wove through the green trees of spring. After a few minutes, he came upon an empty bench.

Seating himself, he looked up through the greenery and began to speak ... out loud, yet faintly, "Denise, I wanted you to be the first to know. I landed a job with Saty Financial. Can you believe it? I hope you are proud of me. I wish you were sitting with me here in this pretty park. It has trees like we had near Traver's Table. Hope you remember. The only thing though, it's not raining. I miss you, Denise, more than ever.

Wish I knew where you are. Now, don't you worry. I won't stop looking for you. I promise."

With a lump in his throat, working a smile to his lips, "Just because I have a $70,000 a year job won't deter me. I'll find you. God, I have to find you."

Kyle was focused on getting off on the right foot at Saty Financial and that meant putting in extra hours with attention to every detail of the job. Kyle had been driving his mother's blue older model car since the beginning of his senior year in college and it was on its last leg. He secured an apartment that was somewhat close to the office on Greenhill Road about a ten minute drive each way. Every bit of Kyle's energy was devoted to the job, except for the few minutes he took each morning and evening to think of, speak to, and pray for ... Denise.

Kyle's first office at Saty Financial was shared with one other analyst, Alban Lowrie who was in his 40's, with a wife and three children. He was cheerful and very helpful to Kyle as he got acclimated to the responsibilities of his new post.

Each day before he left his apartment he placed the framed 5x7 framed picture of Denise in his worn vinyl briefcase. Upon arriving at his office, Kyle would take the photo from his case and place it on the shelf just above his desk. At the end of his work day, the photo was put back in the briefcase. For Kyle, it was a way to take Denise everywhere he went. When he needed a jolt of enthusiasm or energy he had only to look at her photo.

After a few weeks of sharing the same office, Alban began to notice Kyle's ritual with the girl's photograph. He wanted to ask about it but decided not to ask any personal questions of his new colleague. Kyle didn't talk about himself all that much and kept his feelings and details of his life private to himself. He wanted to talk about Denise with Alban. When someone is such a centerpiece of your life, you just have to talk about that person with someone. Kyle just wasn't ready to open up his life to anyone.

Kyle learned his assigned tasks quickly and just as rapidly mastered them, but what drew the attention of all his colleagues and upper management was the genuineness of his demeanor with clients. Time and again clients would go out of their way to offer kudos about Kyle to top Saty Financial officials, noting his charming manner and sincerity in meeting the needs of clients, the least of which was increasing their personal capital.

Chapter 35

Love is not An Emotion ... It's An Act of Will

The months on the job turned into years. Mr. Saty, the CEO and the upper management of the firm recognized the talent and drive of Kyle and incremental promotions came his way on a regular basis. Now in his 7th year of employment at Saty Financial, Kyle had his own office and Alban had been transferred over to Human Resources. It was a snowy day in Philadelphia and most of his appointments were being postponed. Kyle with a temporary lull in his nonstop schedule found himself just staring at Denise's photo, the regular default for his eyes. Alban chanced to walk by Kyle's office and looked in to say hello to his colleague who was looking upward at the photo above his desk.

"Kyle, we've known each other for a while and every day I drop in on you you take out a picture of someone from your briefcase and put it on the shelf. Then when you leave, you always take it with you. Kyle, I have to ask ... who is that person?"

Kyle stood up and tried to consider his words. He took the photo in his hands, looked lovingly at it with a smile and then looking at Alban said, "Alban I would like you to meet Denise."

With that, Kyle turned the picture towards Alban. There was no easy way to explain who she was, so he simply said, "Denise is my heart", as Kyle fought off an intermittent build-up of his tears. Alban saw Kyle's facial muscles tense and his eyes fill and immediately apologized for asking.

Kyle offered a soft wave with his right hand as if to say that everything was ok, but he was surprised in himself that the mere mention of Denise in a conversation brought such intense emotion forward. Other than his talks with Denise in abstentia when he was alone, Kyle realized that this was the first time he had a conversation about her with anyone since his junior year in college with Mr. Belton.

Alban looked at his young colleague and had a slew of questions just waiting to be asked, but viewing the usually demure Kyle displaying such high emotions, he opted to back away from the topic at hand.

Kyle returned to his desk still shaken by the impromptu chat with Alban and looking to the heavens, whispered the words, "God, help me find her".

A whirlwind of energy in his profession, Kyle took time to join civic organizations in Philadelphia, earning a reputation as one of the up and coming stars in the financial community. His firm paid for his graduate work and Kyle was fast tracked to earn his MBA. He accomplished all of this with a humility and leadership style that provided credit to his co-workers. When he designed a plan that led to a large monetary outcome for a client and his firm, he would go out of his way to write a congratulatory memo to each person who had any part of the victory, whether it was an accountant, support staff, or a technician.

Whatever Kyle achieved in his working career, he always lifted others up with him with every step. Kyle called it, "Lift While Climbing".

Kyle received a significant bump in his salary after just two years and was promoted to the position of Senior Estate Financial Manager. Professionally his life could not be moving along much better, but he was incomplete, something was missing. Although his circle of associates and friends had grown since college, Kyle maintained a low-profile social life, usually declining invitations to parties and social gatherings. Although he had received overtures of receptivity from young ladies to dating, Kyle could not break through the threshold of a common objection to ask someone out. No matter how attractive, intelligent or alluring the woman might be, Kyle would always find just enough incompatible not to ask.

Kyle's professional life was his focal point, working long hours with a resulting string of notable achievements. Kyle had bought a home in Balacynwyd, an affluent township and paid an interior decorator to furnish it for him.

Each year he would return to his hometown with a dual purpose. He would visit his mother's grave ... and he would seek out any person who might have knowledge of the whereabouts of Denise. On each visit to his hometown, he would drop in on his former high school, walking the hallways where Denise walked. He would go to the school library where Denise once met with him. Most importantly, he would walk to Traver's Table, sit there remembering that rainy day and talk to Denise as if she was really sitting next to him.

Chapter 36

A Time to Celebrate

One morning just before his 29th birthday, Kyle entered his office, and as he had done daily since his first day with the firm placed Denise's photo on the shelf above his desk. Just then Alban now working in Human Resources, who occupied an office down the hall from Kyle, came rollicking in past Kyle's support staff and proclaimed, "Kyle, Mr. Saty, himself, wants to see you".

Kyle looked at Alban quizzically, "Why are <u>you</u> informing me of this? What does Human Resources have to do with a request for a meeting with Mr. Saty and me?"

"Look Kyle ... I take orders just like you. So I am just informing you that Mr. Saty, the boss, the owner, the man ... wants the pleasure of your company ..... at 9:30 am!"

Kyle thanked Alban for his diligence and prepared to take the elevator up to the top floor to the office of Mr. Saty, CEO of the firm. Before leaving his desk Kyle looked up at Denise's photo and hoped he would have something good to share with her when he returned.

Upon arriving at the epulent corner office on the top floor, Mr. Saty's, executive assistant, Ryan welcomed Kyle, asked him to be seated and wait for just a few minutes as Mr. Saty finished a conference call.

Kyle hadn't been called in for an audience with the illustrious Mr. Saty in almost a year and that brief meeting was to introduce him to a new client.

Seated on a Chippendale bamboo chair, Kyle waited for

five, then ten minutes as he was starting to wonder if this meeting was for something of a negative nature. Finally, Ryan told Kyle that Mr. Saty would see him now.

As Kyle entered Mr. Saty's enormous office he saw many of his colleagues standing around the perimeter with Saty himself seated at the end of the long conference table in the middle of the room.

Saty asked Kyle to be seated at the opposite end of the table as Kyle looked around to see some smirks on the faces of his assembled co-workers. Kyle knew something was up, but he decided to maintain a serious demeanor and play along.

Saty rose from his seat and spoke, "Kyle, as President and CEO of Saty Financial it is my distinct pleasure to inform you that you have been selected as the recipient of the Ragsdale Award by the Institute of Financial Professionals of America as the top financial wealth management advisor in the country for this year."

With that announcement, the assembled persons broke out into applause and laudatory shouts.

Mr. Saty was not quite done with his announcements. "Kyle, the firm is proud of your work and we have all benefitted by your leadership and innovation, thus I am authorized to offer you the position of Director of Analytics for Saty Financial. What say you?"

With more clapping and glad tidings, Kyle accepted the offer. After a short period of hand shaking and congratulatory hugs from colleagues, he returned to his office and closed the door. Taking down the photo of Denise, Kyle kissed it and told her what had just happened. He spoke to her as ever just as if she was right in front of him, "Denise you won't believe what happened to me just now and it wouldn't have happened if not for you. I wish you were really here so we could celebrate together. You know that "happy" is not really happy without you."

Later that day a financial reporter with a photographer from the city's largest newspaper and a camera crew and reporter from one of Philadelphia's television stations came to Kyle's office to interview him on the occasion of this national award. The questions from the journalists were mostly about his work in the financial industry, but they eventually got around to a request for information relative to his family. During the interview, Kyle explained that he had no living family. Then the television reporter spotted the photo above his desk and with cameras rolling and asked Kyle who the girl was in the photo.

Kyle smiled and just said, "Someone too special for words".

The TV reporter followed up her question with another, "Is that your girlfriend, your intended?"

Kyle could only smile and say, "She is my heart".

The journalist laughed and asked no more questions about the photo, but the question, the photo, and Kyle's response were on film.

Kyle was invited for celebratory cocktails and dinner at the Four Seasons that evening by a group of his colleagues, but he graciously declined. He looked forward to the serenity of his home, time to thank God for his blessings of the day ... oh, and a little talk with Denise.

As he drove home his mind drifted to recollections of his mother, all that she had taught him and how she might have reacted if she were alive to hear of his blessings of today.

No matter what his mother faced in life with all of the hardships and saving every penny that Kyle might have money for a college education, all she did was give thanks to God. It was that integrity of her every day life that taught Kyle to be humble and forever wary of an ego out of control. He called to mind the one piece of scripture that Avril had taped onto her dressing table. It was the basis for her emphasis on teaching about "love" to her son. It was burned on his soul and as he turned into his driveway he spoke the scripture, 1st Corinthians 13:13, "And now there remain: faith, hope, love, these three; but the greatest of these is love."

Before he parked his car, Kyle thanked God for the incredible blessings of the day and expressed his belief in the one true God and His promises.

Entering his home, Kyle sat in his dining room and spoke aloud his prayer of faith, hope, and love. "God, today you showered your divine favor down upon me. I did not seek these things, but in receiving them I know I must now serve you in some manner through them. With all that you have given me this day, I ask that you grant the desire of my heart. Please let me find Denise and let love manifest in that discovery. Amen!"

Chapter 37

Forever Closer

In the small township, some 90 minutes away from Kyle's home in Balacynwyd, a 30 year old woman was preparing to close up the gift store she managed after a most productive day of sales and the promise for ever better times ahead. As she went through the day's receipts in her small office, a flat screen television attached to the wall above her was on with the sound turned down, but not completely off. She was primarily concerned about the next day's weather as it often affected customer traffic.

The channel's afternoon anchor team reviewed some of the national events of the day and then cut to one of their correspondents covering "a proud day for one Philadelphia based financier ..."

The reporter, standing outside of the Saty Financial Building began the story announcing Kyle's name and the award he had won. The woman trying to pay attention to her book-keeping kept right on working, and hardly paid attention to the story, but mentally recalled she once knew a boy named Kyle. She looked up at the screen for an instant and saw a man being interviewed ... nothing worth watching. The face was familiar in a remote way, but she dropped her attention back onto the receipts of the day. Suddenly, realizing who this "might be" she did a double-take, snapping her attention back to the screen.

With her eyes widening in disbelief, she saw his name scrolling under the video and frantically pressed the volume button on the remote to hear the rest of the story. Only a matter of seconds remained in the television report as she remembered the boy who just became a man on the television screen right before her eyes.

With the television story over and the announcers moving on to sports and weather, she got up from her desk, very moved by thoughts of Kyle and what he rekindled in her memory.

Her work completed at the gift store, she locked up the building and got in her car for the drive to her apartment. Closing the car door, she flipped up the cover on the vanity mirror on the sun visor. Looking into the mirror she brushed back her hair with her fingers that had fallen onto her forehead during the long day. Peering into the mirror she thought of what her appearance was when last Kyle had seen her.

At that moment she felt especially alone. It had been 12 years since she was a vibrant member of her school's student body, voted Prettiest Girl in the senior class. "Where had her life gone?" she wondered. Shrugging off this little period of self-pity, she got her thoughts back on Kyle. She remembered his infinite kindness, all the phone time when he just listened to her, and especially that terrible day when Frank had humiliated her in public and Kyle expecting to drive her home ended up driving her many miles out of town at her request on Route 222 to a farm. How often she thought about that day.

Any recollection of Kyle was made sweeter by recalling the walk in the rain to Traver's Table and his recitation of a poem, the remnants of which are a crumbled piece of paper from that day still stuffed in a drawer in her dresser.

Later than evening as she prepared a modest dinner for herself, she dismissed a passing idea of contacting Kyle at his place of business. She mused, "I don't need to feel any more crappy should he not remember me".

The next morning arrived a little earlier than usual for Denise. The alarm clock was hardly necessary after years of rising early for her job, and she had more than a few different places of employment in the last decade. She showered, dressed and drove to the coffee shop three blocks away. Everything was strictly routine.

Parking on the side of the coffee shop, she walked pass the metal newspaper racks just outside of the entrance. All the Philadelphia and local papers were stacked for purchase. Taking a quick glance at the headlines, she was stopped in her tracks. There on the front page of Philadelphia's most prestigious paper was a photo of Kyle ... "that Kyle" ... sitting at his desk. She grabbed a copy of the newspaper and went inside to pay for it along with a coffee.

Rushing to get back to her car for the ten minute drive to her place of business, she almost got into an accident, while looking over at the passenger seat where the newspaper was thrown. She couldn't take her eyes off of the photo on the front page.

Upon arriving, she hurriedly ungated the store front making it ready for business when the store opened. She placed her bag, coffee and the newspaper on the small desk and then went about her normal process of taking care of the tasks necessary for daily business, but she had to get to the newspaper.

With all duties completed, she opened her coffee and viewed the front page of the newspaper. She looked at every detail of Kyle's photo and then one small detail caught her attention. Just above Kyle's smiling face, there was a framed photo ..."Oh My God," she screamed ... "That's ME!"

Astonished and rather confused at the sight of her graduation picture from high school on the front page of the Philadelphia paper, she decided she would have to call Kyle. She now concluded, there is no way he wouldn't remember me because **my picture** was on his desk.

The question she could not answer is ... "WHY ... Why was my picture on his desk"?

Chapter 38

Kyle's Blessing

The morning following the announcement of the award and subsequent promotion, Kyle awoke, opening the cream and gold curtains that covered the French doors, leading to the second floor deck outside his bedroom. Standing before the glass doors, he witnessed the overcast skies and the slightest pater of raindrops on the Mahogany wood deck. Any hint of rain would usually evoke an introspection of Denise, but on this morning Kyle opened the French doors with rain dampening the shiny wood and spoke to her. "Denise, we start a new day and I hope where ever you are you see the same clouds and feel the same rain. I don't know why, but I sense you closer to me than you have been in years. Denise, you have always been my every day miracle, my blessing. May God take care of you and bring you to me."

Two hours later, entering the office building the next morning, everyone from security guards to co-workers to people he did not know, offered congratulations on the award and made comments about how good Kyle looked on television. Kyle who did not watch much television had not seen the news broadcast the previous evening or this morning. It seemed everyone else had.

Wanting to see what everyone seemed to have seen but him, Kyle made a hasty about face, exited the building, walked around the corner to the newsstand and there he saw his photo planted on the front page of the morning's newspaper. He had hoped the media would not have put so much importance on his blessing, but good stories are hard to find and the print and electronic media boys and girls were not tardy in singing his praises.

It was quite a start to the new day. He hoped the felicitations would die down quickly so he could get some work done.

Kyle's support staff for two years was Jesse and Jarom, two young and energetic young men just a few years younger than Kyle. They were exceptionally loyal to him and met Kyle's work demands and then some. They never asked too many questions, or over stepped their bounds of professionalism, but both understood the immense degree of sensitivity Kyle possessed and the unspoken love buried within his heart.

On this the day after his promotion to the post of Director of Analytics for Saty Financial, both Jesse and Jarom were a tad giddy at the prospect of moving up in company status and paid grade with their immediate manager, Kyle. As can happen when people get a little too happy and giggly, both were getting a bit loose with their words.

As Kyle was walking to his office from the elevator he heard Jesse and Jarom speaking together with Jarom drolly asking Jesse, "Hey, we'll be getting new offices. Do you think the photo on his desk will be getting a new frame?" Jesse replied, "The way he cares for that picture, <u>whoever it is</u>, Kyle will probably frame it in gold."

Jesse and Jarom had their backs turned and did not notice Kyle's approach.

Kyle came up from behind them, earnestly interjecting, "Gentlemen, I appreciate your joyful disposition and anticipatory posture, but I ask you to refrain from comments relative to the young lady's photo upon my desk. This is a topic of a personal nature and despite your perceptions, whatever they might be, humorous discourse relative to the photo is not appropriate."

Having been summarily rebuked, Jarom and Jesse retreated to their offices. As they turned to leave, Kyle in an unaccustomed moment of un-smiling spontaneity and candor, "By the way, my devoted staff, the young lady's name is DENISE ... D -E-N-I-S-E. That name for me has reverence, you will please note that for the future."

With that, Kyle asked Jesse to screen his calls, unless it was something of an urgent nature as he was not to be disturbed.

The calls from well-wishers and clients were a steady stream of lights and rings on the two phone lines that led to Kyle's office and Jesse did what was asked and cordially took messages.

At the gift store with rain increasing in the streets of the sleepy town, there were no customers in sight. On this day as store manager she hoped there would be no customers, so she could be alone with her thoughts and the tug and pull of the decision to call Kyle.

With her coffee all but untouched and newspaper with Kyle's picture ... and hers, lying directly in front of her, she opened the internet to get the general telephone number of Saty Financial in Philadelphia. The company's website came right up and on the right, an icon, "contact us".

Trying not to consider what to say if she reached Kyle, she keyed the numbers. After two rings, she heard an automatic message, "You have reached Saty Financial, LLC. Thank you for your call. If you know the extension of the party you wish to contact, please dial it now, or please dial "O" for our operator."

She dialed for the operator.

The operator answered and asked for the name of the department or the person she wished to contact. Taking a deep breath she spoke Kyle's full name. The operator casually mentioned, "He is a very popular man today. Please hold. I will connect you".

Jesse answered, "Good morning, how can I help you?"

The girl, now a woman, who long ago could call Kyle at any time, "May I speak to Kyle?"

Jesse responded, "Thank you for your call, it is very important to us, however, Kyle is very busy at the moment. May I take a message?"

In a brief moment of disappointment, then almost saying

that she didn't want to leave a message, she said ..."Sir would you tell Kyle that Denise called."

As if a stick of dynamite just went off in his head, Jesse raised the volume of his voice, "Did you say your name was Denise?"

In an instant of total indecision, Jesse told her, "Ma'am, Denise, please hold, don't go away. Give me a minute. Please hold!"

Jesse put the phone down, running around the corner to Kyle's office. Upon arriving, Jesse saw the inside maple door to his office closed. Risking another dressing down, he knocked on the door and not waiting to be told to enter, he opened the door.

Kyle gave Jesse a look and restated, "What did you not understand about the words, "not to be disturbed".

Jesse not able to bridle his tangled reactions, "Kyle ... listen ... I'm sorry to bother you, but there is this woman on the phone. She says her name is Denise."

Just hearing the name, Kyle jerked his head back, then spoke with matter-of-fact calmness, "Jesse there are thousands of women named Denise. C'mon now."

Jesse not knowing what more to say or do, "Kyle ... there is a woman on the phone who is holding. Her name is Denise. Do you want me to take a message?"

The sound of just her name from another human being's mouth was too powerful to overcome for Kyle. He raised his palms to his shoulders in momentary surrender, "Alright, Jesse put this woman through to me."

Jesse flew back to his desk and pressed the hold button in hopes she was still there, "Miss are you still there?"

She answered, "Yes, I have been patient. I'm here."

"I will put you through to him now."

THE WORLD STOPPED ... THE LOST WAS FOUND.

Line one on Kyle's office phone lit up on his desk as the phone rang.

Before he pressed the button and picked up the receiver, he took a deep breath, not permitting himself to believe that this was her. He composed himself, assuming his most professional opening salutation.

"Good morning, this is Kyle, may I help you?

A momentary pause and then, he heard, "Hiiiiiiiiiiiiiiiiii."

Instantly, Kyle's entire body, mind, and spirit were transformed. He was in a different place.

His breath was that of a desert wind, but his eyes could not hold back the tears.

Kyle swallowed and whispered, "Denise?"

She followed, "Kyle?"

He murmured again, "Denise?"

As she spoke so many years ago in another reality and time, "Kyle, can you talk?"

With that, Kyle dissolved into tears, an outpouring of emotion unequaled in his collective memory.

Denise heard his sniffles and gasp of breath, "Kyle, is that really you? Are you alright?"

Kyle was unable to control much of his emotion and his words started to bypass all mature filters of comportment. He spoke without encumbrance from his surging heart, "Denise ... don't leave me. Don't go away again".

Denise was puzzled by Kyle's words, unable to grasp their meaning. It was all too much ... too sudden.

Kyle gathered himself and slowed the moment down. "Denise, I have been looking for you since forever. I looked everywhere and called anyone who might have known where you were. There is so much to talk with you about."

Kyle heard Denise's voice crack over the phone. Now they were both in tears.

"Kyle", Denise tried to explain, "a lot has happened since high school. Most of it not so good for me, at least. We don't have time now. I have a business to run. May I call you tonight?"

"Denise, I cannot let you get off the phone unless you give me your phone number," Kyle countered.

Denise gave Kyle her cellphone number and Kyle returned his.

Denise was smiling on her end of the phone; she shared

a small but important fact. "Kyle, do you know what? ... It's **raining** here."

Kyle, who had started his day in the acknowledgement that rain and Denise were ultimately connected simple replied, "... of course it is."

Suddenly, Kyle heard that distinctive Denise laugh that was burned on his heart all those years ago.

Kyle inquired, "And what is so funny, young lady?"

Denise looking down at the newspaper in front of her, "Why is my picture on your desk? It's on the front paper of the newspaper. I haven't seen or talked to you in over a decade. Are you using it as a paperweight? What does your wife say about that?"

Kyle smiled and quietly explained, "Denise I cannot tell you right now why your picture goes with me wherever I go, but I will in time if you allow me. All I can tell you now is that the picture you gave me at Christmas time in high school is in the only place it was always meant to be."

"Oh, by the way," he added, "I'm not married. Are you?"

Denise didn't answer right away. "No, no ... I am not married ... anymore."

Kyle had been drained by these few minutes of renewal on the phone with "The Girl". He could not know what Denise was experiencing on the other end of the phone. He could only hope it was something positive.

There was a knock on Kyle's office door. It was Jarom reminding him of a scheduled appointment in ten minutes. Denise hearing the voice in the background suggested that he better go and that she also had to get back to her work responsibilities.

Kyle did not want to end this phone conversation. He never wanted to end any of the phone calls with Denise from back in high school. Some things never change and never will. Denise's tone softened, whispering, "I will call you tonight."

Both were at a loss to find words to place an end to this brief talk of reconnection, so they both simply said "bye".

There would be no meaningful work from Kyle after the

call from Denise. He met his obligations with two clients but otherwise sat at his desk in profound silence.

The world had just stopped for Kyle. The lost was found. Denise was alive. Denise was there, somewhere, close enough to read a Philadelphia newspaper, too far from him now, and no distance in miles would be too far to keep her from him.

Chapter 39

Evening Rain

Upon arriving home at 7:00 pm, Kyle was filled with wonderment having heard the voice of the one girl who changed the direction of his life, but there was a sense of partial fulfillment. Denise was within a phone call's distance from him. His prayers to find her had been answered, but they were incomplete. Kyle who could be single-minded in his professional life to the point of obsessive now focused on paving an avenue of trust over the telephone that might result in seeing Denise face to face.

As Kyle waited for his cellphone to ring, there was a veil of memories that covered him. Since he first saw Denise in high school, they only had been in each other's company a matter of hours, yet no person in his life had caused such a dramatic shift in his personal development, altering the course of his life. Denise's mere acts of kindness that included her smiling with eyes directed at him gave life to his hidden gifts and ignited a fire of belief within Kyle that all things were possible. So many times during that 11th grade year Kyle would ask himself, "Imagine a girl like Denise, talking to a boy like me."

Kyle's vivid remembrance of their tender moment together at a remote farm off the highway unlocked a door to the depth of his heart, but unbeknownst to Kyle Denise held the only key. She still holds the key and no one will ever be able to unlock that door again, but Denise.

Kyle's mercurial academic rise over the last two years of high school was the direct result of Denise in his life. She was the perfect catalyst, "perfect in everyway" to Kyle. Denise and Kyle rarely discussed classes, grades or long term plans for the future, but by finding his ways to love, Kyle was raised up, establishing a foundation of consistent achievement over the next four years of his college life. He had often looked back on his dramatic transformation from a scared isolated 15 year old boy to a dean's list performer at the university, but the events of the last few days in his professional career brought further credence that Denise was the gift that keeps on giving.

The waiting for the phone to ring ended at 8:50 pm. As Kyle answered, a soft elongated "Hiiiiiiiiiiiiiiiii," filled his ear. It was Denise ... that Denise ... the only Denise.

Their first few minutes on the phone were a frantic back and forth and words, laughs, and general catch-up. They both uttered the same phases, "so good to hear your voice. ... I can't believe it's really you."

With preliminary joviality out of the way, Kyle stated what was chiefly on his mind, "Denise, I have to see you. I must see you."

A momentary silence and Denise responded, "I don't think that is a good idea right now."

"But why?" Kyle shot back.

"A lot has happened Kyle, too much to get into."

Kyle heard a change in her voice and offered a change of topic, "Denise, so tell me what happened after you graduated high school. I know you and your family moved out of town that summer after you graduated. That was one of the last things you told me before you disappeared."

Denise snapped back, "I didn't disappear. We moved and then we moved again as my father was transferred for his job to Canada."

"I'm sorry Denise. I didn't mean to infer anything, but after our last conversation in June, the year you graduated I never heard from you again", Kyle offered apologetically.

Denise was suddenly overtaken by memories of a long ago past with bad memories that she did not want to be rehashed, not now at least. Apprehension, panic clouded her voice, "Kyle,

I gotta go. We'll talk some other time ... maybe." With that, Denise hung up.

Kyle was stunned. Did he say the wrong thing, ask the wrong question, push too hard?

Kyle had heard fear in Denise's voice and began to dial her number, but thought it prudent to wait for a while. After an hour, Kyle picked up his cellphone and began to dial Denise's number, but again stopped not wanting to be hung up on, again.

With a busy schedule planned for the next day that included a civic organization luncheon where he was to be the featured speaker, Kyle wrapped up his confused thoughts and headed to bed. Lying awake, gazing at the ceiling he could find no peace.

Sometime after 1:00 am, his cellphone went off. He stumbled jumping out of bed to get to his phone that was on the dresser. Sliding the accept button on his phone he heard, "I'm sorry."

"Denise, please, don't hang up again, please," Kyle begged.

Denise's voice wavered as she was clearly crying. "Kyle, I'm sorry for hanging up on you. I wanted so much to talk to you, but it is painful to talk about what my life has been."

Denise asked, "Can you talk for a few minutes?"

"I'm here with you and for you," Kyle offered, "Talk to me".

Denise took a deep breath and commenced to tell Kyle of the often challenging events that dotted her life since high school. She explained how her father's job required them to move from city to city with a long stay in Canada. During that tenure in Canada, Denise's mother died from a heart ailment.

Next, Denise confirmed what she told Kyle in high school, She decided to go to the same college as Frank. Kyle, just hearing the name Frank again, brought about the dreaded prospect that he might be in for hours of listening to tales about Frank.

Taking in her every word, Denise explained that after her freshman year in college, she and Frank got married. Denise wasted no time in stating that the marriage was a mistake from the beginning. Frank was abusive, calling her terrible names, and striking her on a few occasions. The marriage lasted only seven months before they were divorced.

Unable to afford college on her own, Denise went to her father for financial help, but his growing health problems required him to leave his job, so she was forced to withdraw from college.

Denise moved in with her father and subsequently became his care giver. He died from prostate cancer 3 years ago.

Kyle could only listen as Denise recounted the most agonizing of details of each one of these episodes in her life.

Denise wanted Kyle to know all of this information.

Kyle who had become more philosophical over the years, and was just as comforting as ever, suggested that these events are all part of what life brings on us, "Nobody has an obstacle free life. We all have trials that we have to overcome, but God never allows a problem to stand before us that He doesn't give us the tools and ability to overcome."

Denise was taken by the wisdom of Kyle, a trait that he was too young to demonstrate when he only listened to her over the phone.

Kyle could wait no longer, "Denise I want to see you. We need to meet and talk."

Denise immediately backed away from any suggestion of meeting, "Why do you want to see me? We can talk over the phone if you want."

"I have wanted to find and see you for over 12 years. I will go anywhere to see you, Denise. Nothing is more important to me," pleaded Kyle.

Kyle not wanting to push too hard, evoking a quick hang up again by Denise, asked, "Can we talk about this tomorrow?"

Denise looking at her bedroom clock, reported, "Kyle, do you know it is 3:45 am?"

Kyle had no idea how the time on the phone with Denise had passed so quickly. He remembered his lengthy work schedule of the next day and realized he best get some sleep or at least try.

"I'm sorry for keeping you so long," lamented Denise.

"I wouldn't have traded it for anything," responded a thankful Kyle.

He asked, "Denise before we say goodbye, will you let me explain something to you?"

"Go ahead. I've been doing all the talking for hours. It's your turn."

Kyle gathered in his collective feelings of the night, "Denise, you may not understand it yet, and maybe you never will, but the things I have been able to achieve in my life so far are in large part because of you and only you. We will always have a lot to say to each other, but we need to sit in front of each other and speak with words."

Kyle ended with, "... Denise ... I need you and you know what? ... I think you need me."

"I will call you tomorrow," submitted Denise, "... unless you have better things to do."

Kyle could only smile, "Good night my Denise."

"Byeeeeeeeeee," in perfect Denise style.

Chapter 40

Voices Before Meeting

When of high school age with hardly more than the demands of homework, and the daily family routine, Denise and Kyle would talk over the phone for a half hour, maybe an hour. Now as single adults with only the necessities of life and the preparation for the ensuing day's work, they spoke into the early morning. It was a phone call for catch-up, a time to listen and try to understand the filling that stuffed the years between them. Whatever topics they might share in a next phone call would build on the previous evening's conversation.

For Denise, the day after that late evening call to Kyle was one of introspection. She thought about Kyle constantly and could not understand why after all these years he could possibly feel the way he said he does in holding her responsible for the good things that have happened to him. She reflected on those limited memories. We were friends ... We talked over the phone... We never saw each other socially or even hung out in school ... We never dated. Maybe he is confusing me with someone else.

Opps! Then she remembered that day when she asked Kyle to drive her home and they ended up pulled over near a lake on a farm. Yes, she recalled the sudden tenderness, the gentle affection they shared. All at once after all these years that event was worthy of her most comprehensive remembrance. Denise placed her fingers to her mouth, recalling the featherlike feel of Kyle's fingers on her lips. She remembered the soothing voice, the whispers. All at once, Denise had a sense of guilt

147

that she had never thought of those moments in just that way before ...or of Kyle as something other than just a shy thoughtful boy she once knew.

Denise searched her memory. She worried, what else had she chose to forget about Kyle or put away on a shelf of distracting memories? Of all the phone conversations they had back then, what might Kyle have said that she disregarded or just blatantly ignored?

Denise searched her feelings and she was afraid. Maybe she better not talk to Kyle anymore. After all, he's got his life going well, and I have ... my life.

It was a fairly busy day at the shop for Denise as buyers were in to suggest new lines of merchandise and a soon-to-be bride and her mother were in select gifts for the wedding party. In between each fold of activity, Denise fought the need to think of Kyle.

Over at Saty Financial, the new Director of Analytics was trying to finish up pending work with Jarom and Jesse while making a list of priorities for the transition to the new position. Every so often Kyle would stand and look out his office window and think of Denise, something that did not escape the notice of Jarom.

Jarom, a charming and devoted assistant to Kyle who stood six foot, three inches came up beside Kyle as he stood at the window. Jarom in a bold act of kindness had taken Kyle's photo of Denise from its shelf. Jarom placed his left hand on Kyle's shoulder, "Kyle you forgot this," and handed the photo to Kyle.

Kyle looked up at his aide-de-camp, pursing his lips with a nod, "How did you know I was thinking about her," he asked.

"Hey boss, when aren't you thinking about her?"

Kyle looked down at the photo of "The Girl" and muttered, "I talked to her."

Jarom looked over at Kyle, "... but did you see her."

"No, I asked to see her, but she changed the subject," Kyle responded.

Jarom fired back at his diminutive boss, "You mean to stand there and even suggest that you are going to hold for that from (Jarom grabbed the photo from Kyle and shoved it right in front of Kyle's face.) ... DENISE?"

Kyle broke out in a wide smile, something his staff rarely saw from him.

Jarom more than acknowledged the Kyle smile, "Jesse, look at this smile. If one mention of the woman's name can get our Kyle to smile like that, we must get these two together."

Kyle returned to his desk, but remembered one of the last things his mother imparted to him that was sparked by Jarom's call to action, "Love is not an emotion, it is an act of will."

Seeing Denise was something he had prayed about. Kyle knew that relying on his emotions alone was not sufficient. He needed to find the right words to ask Denise to meet him.

He wanted Denise's will and his will to be a harmonious singular "act of will".

Chapter 41

A Time to Act

In his young life, especially in the last ten years, Kyle had learned not to wait when opportunity's doorway showed a ray of light from which to proceed. Kyle did not know where Denise resided, but he sensed where her heart lived. In the conversation of this coming night, he would offer to invite Denise to a place where her wondrous heart would be at home, at peace, removed from any and all iniquities of the past.

As the final rim of the day's sun slipped into dusk, Kyle's cellphone erupted in sound. The phone had not left his hands since he had arrived home from the office.

The first sound, the "hiiiiiiiiiiiiiiiiiiiiiii," made wider the opening of his heart.

Before Denise had the slightest tiny window of time to say anything more Kyle interrupted her.

"Denise, I have something that must be said first," announced Kyle.

A focused Denise would have no first word from Kyle, "You had better let me say something first before you say something first."

Kyle replied, "No, young lady, I choose to begin the dialogue."

Denise loudly rejoined with, "Let us agree to an impasse and agree to talk at the same time when I count three."

Kyle, a skilled negotiator, but at a rare disadvantage with "the girl", barked out, "AGREED."

Silence prevailed for a few seconds as Denise reminded Kyle, "I will count to three. Neither one of us may speak more than three words. Are we in agreement?"

Kyle, feeling like he finally had some leverage as silly as this seemed to be answered, "AGREED".

Denise commenced the count ... "one ... two ... three".

Together, with the boldness of a Beethoven symphony, they both yelled, "**LET'S MEET!**"

A hesitation pause, then shrieks of laughter erupted from Denise and Kyle. No matter what they did to quell the convulsing giggles, they just couldn't stop.

Soon, with deep breathes and the acknowledgement that something special had just occurred between them, there was calm. After sharing their addresses, they learned that they were approximately 70 minutes away from each other.

Their next topic was the when, the where, and details of an attitudinal approach that Denise insisted upon. Denise had been through her share of negative experiences with men and thought rationally about what their mindset should be.

As Kyle was getting wrapped up in a haze of romance and intemperate joy, Denise was the equilibrium. Kyle recommended a number of locations for them to meet from inner city Philadelphia to the Poconos. Denise expressed the need for them to slow down and requested that they have a common sense approach to meeting for the first time.

Denise insisted that they do not approach the meeting as a "date-date". "Let's not put any pressure on either of us. You haven't seen me in 12 years. You might take one look at me and go running for the exit. I'm not that 17 year old girl you used to know," explained Denise.

Kyle's words were in full agreement for calm, but inside was an excitement that was years on the boil.

"Let's just take the attitude that this is a meeting "between old friends," proposed Denise.

At this point, Kyle would agree to just about anything for Denise.

With that groundwork established, Kyle asked Denise permission to determine the location of their meeting, promising that it will be safe, elegant and private. Kyle had given Denise no reason to believe that anything he might choose would be considered amorously suggestive.

Kyle needed to ask this question, "Denise, do you feel you can trust me?"

Denise considered that question for a few moments, saying only, "In high school, you were an innocent kid who I did trust. Now, you are a big shot financier who commands the respect of your professional friends. To the extend I can, I trust you, but trust takes time to build."

Kyle assured Denise, I will never let you down and after looking for you for so long I will do nothing to lose you now.

With that understanding, they both agreed to meet on the 12th, two weeks from Saturday. Denise agreed to let Kyle pick the location that was somewhere in the middle of that 70 minute travel time between their homes.

As that seminal phone call came to a close that evening, Kyle and Denise initiated a new round of daily phone calls, sometimes two a day. Their calls leading up to the 12th meeting date were fresh and wonderfully wrapped in smiles and childlike anticipation.

On the 10th of the month, Kyle told Denise that he was sending her a box, scheduled to arrive the next day, called a "Denise Care Package". When she opened it she found a large envelope with an engraved invitation that read:

DENISE

You are cordially invited to attend
"an old friends' meeting"
On the 12th
at the
CASHMERE COUCH RESTAURANT

Denise did not know anything about this restaurant or where it was located, but she knew Kyle was gradually building up their first meeting and would give her all the details at the right time. Kyle's description of the restaurant seemed way over the top for a meeting of old friends, but with each passing day and phone conversation, Denise became enamored by the care that Kyle was placing on every detail. She decided that other than her choice of attire, she would leave all the planning to Kyle.

Chapter 42

Everything Counts

As Kyle settled into his office chair his thoughts were of the meeting with Denise on the 12th.

Denise had brought him to a full examination of his life. Ideals and details of the past and present cascaded in his head. Kyle had learned that in life everything counts. There is no "do over" or "my bad" calls that children and adults often voice. You either acknowledge your victories and defeats in life or you will fail to learn from either. Kyle wanted to do it all correctly on the 12th.

The words of his former high school mentor, Robert kept repeating in his thoughts, like an advertising jingle on the radio, "those who fail to plan, plan to fail". With the inspiration of Denise in his heart, Kyle had adopted that mantra and used it to build an outstanding high school and collegiate career. Kyle had become a fanatic planner in virtually everything he did.

In high school, success in his classes began to turn around in his favor when he paid close attention to details. It became a calming factor for him when he discerned that little things matter from how he wrote his name on a test paper to where and when he did his studying at home.

Unfortunately, Kyle did not apply this attitude of "everything counts" to personal relationships. Deferring from dating in high school, Kyle had spent time with a few girls in college, none of which drew his continuing attentions. Although he kept his focus on the academic tasks at hand at the university, he would, as every young man does, allow his eyes to be pulled in the direction of attractive females. For better or worse, the impact of Denise on his heart as a standard by which all girls were to be measured could not be overcome. He did not dwell on an obsessive comparison, but it was always present. Periodically, a girl of some charm and beauty would stand before him or sit beside him in class. He would consider asking her out on a date, but inevitably he would think ... "Yes, she is very nice, intelligent and pretty, (pause), but she is no Denise".

With him attaching so much importance to this meeting with Denise, he could not ignore the formula that had worked so well for him.

Kyle was trying to remain calm in the highly emotional caldron of his heart on the precipice of meeting her. Kyle asked God for help, praying in Philippians 4:6, "Do not be anxious about anything, but in everything by prayer and supplication with thanksgiving let your requests be made known to God."

There would be no "do over" or "reset button" for him. Although this was not a life and death event, it sure felt like it to him. Kyle wanted this wedge of time, hours that could prove to be inadequate, no matter the outcome, to demonstrate and express all that Denise meant to him. If he could make it almost perfect, just maybe all the dreams and desires he held that were wrapped up in his heart for this young woman, would have a possibility of realization.

He knew he was placing extra pressure on himself, but he could not temper his expectations. This was so different in every way possible, from anything others had said about "love". Kyle realized how overwhelming it had become. It was as though he had no control over his heart. There was a runaway train inside of him and he was powerless to slow it down, let alone stop it.

He thought and thought about this apparent earthquake tremoring inside of him. He asked himself all the questions, seeking some logical answers. When did this all start? Why, after all these years, is there such power in just the saying of her name, "Denise"? The recent telephone calls with her were a renewal, a fresh coat of paint on all of these intense emotions that Kyle kept tucked in his gut all these years. However, the words that were said were insignificant compared to the tidal wave of passion brought forth by just the sound of her voice and her gentle, "hiiiiiiiiiiiiiiiiiiiiiii".

This was to be a moment in life that he thought would, and could never happen, but now, it was right in front of him.

Kyle was a goal setter, but he did not have a definitive goal in meeting Denise, except that he wanted to make their time together special in every way, hopefully leading to a lasting relationship. His attention to detail would never be more personal than for this meeting.

Kyle mapped his route to the Cashmere Couch. It would take just a tad over 40 minutes. The more he considered this ride to Denise, the more he would smile to himself and think it more fitting if he were to walk the distance. Acknowledging that declaration in the deepest recesses of his heart he smiled with a romantic garnish and momentarily considered a biblical pilgrimage of sorts, traveling on foot to get to her. His life had been inalterably changed by this girl ... this woman. It was just as his mother explained to him when he was only 12 ... "There is only ONE".

Whether there was ever to be another time when they would meet, look in each other's eyes, Kyle was fully resolved to the fact that "There <u>was</u> only one and she was Denise". In all of his life, there was never anything he was so sure about than Denise being THE ONE. However, his belief did not have anything to do with what Denise thought about him and that knowledge was not his to have.

The date was set, the 12th, 6:00 pm. As Denise had stated in their telephone call this was not a 'date-date" ... just a meeting of old friends. Naturally, Kyle could not grasp what this cryptic title of a "meeting of old friends" was supposed mean, but he wanted it to be everything it could mean. He began to plan for the event with the care that he planned his professional work, but he recognized that he had no clear goal or outcome for the meeting. He didn't know what to expect or what Denise might have in mind.

Kyle's private life was rarely if ever, shared with his colleagues. Kyle's staffers, Jarom and Jesse, became keenly aware of the re-emergence of "the girl", Denise, in his life in recent days. Unfortunately, Kyle was far too excited about the impending get together to keep it a secret and shared it with them. Kyle found himself preoccupied over this event as few, if any, ever had in his life.

Having told them about the meeting, Jarom, ever the professional suggested certain things he (Jarom) might do to help Kyle prepare. Jarom asked if Kyle would like him to send flowers to the restaurant for Denise. Did he need his tuxedo cleaned, and would Kyle like Jarom to order a limo for that day, so driving is not a concern?"

The offers of assistance from Jarom got Kyle thinking about the little details of the meeting. Kyle had never allowed himself to think in terms of romantic moments and how to make one extra special, but now the time had come and Kyle's creative wheels were turning.

Kyle's head and heart were working in unison and he hatched a plan, starting with a phone call to the general manager of the Cashmere Couch. Kyle decided to spare no expense. He looked within himself for ideas that would demonstrate to Denise how important she was to him. Kyle considered asking Jarom, Jesse, even Mr. Saty himself but knew that for this to be right, he had to do it himself.

Kyle struggled to manage it all in his heart and head. It all seemed so overwhelming. He wondered did every man go through this for a woman?

He had not seen Denise in 12 years. Now, with both of their lives in totally different places, far away from the days of just watching her walk, smile and talk to other students, they were going to meet together.

Kyle never thought of himself as anything more than a confidant of hers. They were alone on only two occasions, the day in the rain at Traver's Table and the long drive on Route 222. Yes, there was the kiss, but from that time forward all

Kyle was, at least in his mind, was someone for Denise to share her thoughts with on the phone.

He wrestled with his memory to recall the details of their talks those many years ago so as to have some basis for a conversation when they met. All he could remember clearly were her lengthy speeches about Frank, and despite all he had done to make her sad, how much she loved him. At that moment he envied Frank.

To be sure both of them had changed, in what ways he could only guess. She sounded exactly as he remembered her voice, even the little earthy giggle was the same. There was happiness all over her voice and that alone wrapped a blanket of joy about Kyle that he had not known. He rationalized that he was no longer that 16 year old boy, enamored with a girl that was so above him in every way.

Kyle found himself preoccupied over the 12th, more than any other event in his life.

In the two weeks prior to their "old friends meeting", the phone calls started earlier in the evening but took on a different mosaic of questions, answers, and anecdotes. Kyle had always been a good listener for Denise and had become used to drinking in every word Denise would say. It never got old or one-sided to him.

However, during these two weeks, before they would see each other, Denise asked Kyle endless questions. During high school, Denise rarely asked him anything deeper than, "How is your mom?"

As the 12th neared Denise wanted to know how Kyle *felt* about many things. She asked about what he felt when they walked to Traver's Table and did he ever miss her after she graduated. Kyle would answer honestly, but would never reveal all that was pent up inside of him for her. Kyle's feelings for Denise were an atomic bomb waiting to be detonated and he had no intention of releasing them over the telephone. There was a deep sensitivity to the phone calls. The tone and texture of Denise's voice was no longer of a carefree girl, but of a thoughtful caring woman.

Denise's life had required that she put up some protective

devices, guarding her feelings and limiting her dreams and aspirations. These few weeks talking with Kyle, she unintentionally, started to unzip her heart, permitting its loving contents to flow out and allow the best of Kyle to pour into her.

Chapter 43

Cashmere Couch

The evening before their "friends meeting", Kyle and Denise talked on the phone as they had each night for a few weeks, but the tenor of the talk was different. Gone from their back and forth phone chat was the customary byplay of fact finding and occasional giggling. On this night Denise was trying to stay relaxed, sitting in her living room on her divan with her feet up clutching a pillow. Some 70 miles away, Kyle was standing before his French doors, looking out over his backyard, watching the night sky. Both were making every effort to keep it light while slipping in an intermittent "... can't wait to see you."

The time they set for their mutual arrival at the Cashmere Couch Restaurant was 6:00 pm, so that they could drive in daylight and give themselves unfettered time to literally *meet each other again* ... after so many years. They had little face to face history, so Kyle and Denise both realized how new and fresh this would all be.

Kyle subtly reminded Denise that he planned a few "meager surprises" and that his attire would be of an elegant formality befitting the years of missed moments and his desire to honor her. When Kyle would talk like this to her about this "friends meeting" it would make her rather nervous. As she had in a previous call a week ago, she pointedly asked Kyle what his attire would be. Kyle told her it was to be formal dinner attire and Denise gently teased, "How are we going to just act like old friends on a couch in that kind of apparel?"

Kyle replied in dismissive fashion, "We'll make it work".

Denise had her own plan as it pertained to wardrobe and wanted to be as attractive as she ever had been. In talking to Kyle in recent weeks she recognized Kyle could be very romantic, despite his assertion that he was a complete novice. Although Denise wanted to keep the night airy and cheerful, she too was susceptible to the romantic haze that seemed to be hanging over them.

As they said goodbye to each other on the phone they were both filled with anticipation for the coming day. There would be a restlessness that kept both of them from easily falling asleep. Kyle had made some unique plans for their meeting and he hoped that his efforts would not make Denise uncomfortable in any way.

Kyle rose early the next day, attempted to pay some bills, but after transposing the amounts on two checks, he realized that any endeavor unrelated to Denise would be futile.

For Denise Saturday usually meant a busy day at the gift shop. On this particular Saturday the only thing on her mind was meeting Kyle and so with her charming best she convinced the owner to give her the day off.

In mid-afternoon, three hours before the planned arrival time at the Cashmere Couch, both Kyle and Denise began their preparations.

Kyle had not shaved for two days, an appearance feature that did not miss the notice of Jarom at the office. Jarom asked Kyle if he had planned to look like a GQ cover boy of 25 years old with a three day growth. Kyle explained that there was a purpose to his roughage and that someday he might explain it to Jarom.

Kyle had learned over the years that if he refrains from shaving even for a day that when he does shave, carefully and slowly, his skin is softer and supple. On this day, Kyle wanted the best face he could muster. He reminded himself ... there was no "do over", so he had to get everything as right as he could.

Denise recognized how different this "meeting" was from any other event in her life. She tried to hold herself back from any expectations, good or bad, but the words that Kyle said to her over the phone, coupled with the years she had spent in disappointment and unfulfilled dreams, made her heart yearn for something magical to occur.

Kyle departed from home over an hour before the time they were to meet. The skies were heavily overcast, but temperatures comfortable. He needed to get there as early as possible to ensure that every little detail he had planned with the cooperation of the general manager was on schedule. Conversely, Denise wanted to take a leisurely drive, free to think, relax and arrive but a few minutes before 6:00 pm. She didn't want to get there before Kyle and she sure didn't want to appear too anxious.

The drive for Kyle was anything but relaxed. The build-up of untallied thoughts of Denise since high school, talking to her photo each day, praying for her reappearance and never having been able to liberate the singular voice in his heart for her, surrounded him.

Recognizing that each moment in life is precious and can never be repeated, no matter how much people try to duplicate events through anniversaries, birthdays, and reunions, this "meeting of old friends", had to last forever in both of their memories. There would be no second opportunity for this first meeting.

The agreed upon 6:00 pm to afford them an unrushed first few minutes, allowing them to breathe together. Neither of them could predict exactly how those opening moments might translate in terms of feelings and words, so eliminating any interference with restaurant staff, servers and sommelier was of importance to Denise and Kyle.

Kyle arrived shortly before 5:15 pm, seeking out the general manager to make sure every planned enhancement and sequence of loving elements would be ready. At 5:30 pm, a long 15 foot white carpet was unfurled from the entrance as two young men sprinkled red rose pedals on the runner. All other arriving patrons were directed to enter through the side doors.

At 5:45 pm the same two young men now dressed in black

dinner jackets stood outside of the front entrance of the Cashmere Couch. Each carried a dozen red long stem roses with an additional single white rose in the middle of each bouquet.

A few moments before 6:00 pm, a red car turned into the parking lot. An elegant woman stepped from its driver side door. As she walked to the entrance Kyle was standing against the large wooden doors that led to the restaurant. Denise was attired in a navy blue full length evening gown with tank straps joined by sheer off-the-shoulder straps that supported a fitted bodice featuring a plunging neckline.

Denise approached the entrance, wondering if this was meant for her or some wedding. Thereupon, the two young men, holding roses, stepped to either side of her and asked in unison, "Do we have the honor of addressing Denise?"

Denise nodded her head. Then looking up she caught her first glance of Kyle who was dressed in a navy blue wide lapel tuxedo.

Kyle took a few steps to Denise and now, after 12 years, they were within inches of each other.

The once shy Kyle now spoke the words he planned to say, "Denise, I would be honored to serve as your escort. May I offer you my arm?"

The enchanting Denise responded, "I would be charmed by your escort, if you will consent to taking my hand in yours."

Try as he might, prepared as he thought he was, he could not hold back the tears that filled his eyes. Denise was already overcome by these few expressions of adoration and friendship. Nothing made sense to Denise at the moment, but everything made sense.

The two dinner-jacketed young men opened the eight foot high wooden carved doors that served as the main entrance with roses in hand as Kyle and Denise entered to the flash of a photographer's camera. Pausing for a second photo to be taken, a gentleman in a white dinner-jacket, bid them welcome and requested that they please follow him.

Their hands ... Kyle's left, Denise's right, came together. Kyle felt the softness of Denise's palm on his, and took a short breath as Denise spoke to him with a grin, "Looks like our hands fit."

They were led up a spiral staircase to the left side of the second flood, covered with closed, floor to ceiling black pleated velvet curtains with gold bunting and tassels. They were asked to wait just outside the curtained area.

The two men with roses stood before them and with one coordinated movement, drew back the black velvet curtains. Before their eyes was a high back couch of red cashmere, trimmed in gold. Behind the kidney shaped couch were more floor to ceiling black velvet curtains.

The two dozen red roses with the one single white rose in each bunch were placed in crystal vases on either end of the couch. A long glass cocktail table was situated in front of their couch.

Kyle bid Denise to be seated on the couch, but Denise slowly shook her head "no". No words were needed for what had to follow.

Standing directly in front of the couch, they stood together, looking into each other's eyes as their arms wrapped about each other. Denise's arms folded about Kyle's neck as Kyle placed his arms around her. Denise wanted to whisper something to Kyle as his ear was pressed against her lips, but all that came out was, "I....."

Kyle held her tight against him as he always had dreamed of doing as their hearts beat as one.

Tears still filled Kyle's eyes with the belief that no two people, but them, could ever hug like this, or would again.

The embrace was both gentle and powerful as neither of them wanted to break its bonds of affection. They stood together coupled in a single hug, slightly moving their faces back to look in each other's eyes.

Words, so plentiful through the utility of a phone, were somehow knotted in their throats and all they could say was what was in their eyes. Swallowing hard, Kyle stole a deep breath, speaking long delayed words, "Denise ...you were perfect ... you are perfect ... and you will always be perfect."

With their eyes sealed in gaze and glory, Kyle and Denise

fought the moment to do something more in their evolving little "first meeting" scene.

Just then one of the dinner-jacketed men asked for permission to enter their curtained room. Once admitted, he held before him a silver tray with four glasses of wine, two red and two white. Approaching Denise and Kyle, "We bid you welcome to the Cashmere Couch. Sir (addressing Kyle), as per your request here are the four wines you wished to taste".

Kyle handed a glass of white wine to Denise and requested she taste it. Denise did so and Kyle handed her the next glass of white wine and then the reds. When all four glasses of wine had been tasted, Kyle asked Denise, "Now, what is your pleasure?"

With the waiter standing before them with the silver tray of wine, the playful Denise squinted at Kyle and said, "You pick". Kyle selected one of the wines and the chosen bottle was opened, breathing and ready for their pleasure within minutes.

Reseated together on the red couch, with their inside legs touching, they began to talk softly about any and all things. Kyle could not believe how she had not changed despite the passing years. Denise peered into Kyle's face and wondered why she never noticed the features of his face and the degree of attractiveness he possessed. In the midst of the conversation, Denise touched Kyle's face and smiling said, "Are you sure you are the same Kyle from high school?"

Kyle responded as if he anticipated the question, "Would you like me to prove it?"

Denise made that scrunched-up smiling face she did many years ago, "Yes, I would like you to prove it."

With that, Kyle spoke the words, *"Dressed in blue, a double hue of cobalt and textured old navy. I couldn't look away, you made my eyes stay. Who was this girl in the hallway? Though postured and slight, an elegant delight, each movement your statement of beauty ...."*

Denise, knowing instantly what those words were and where they came from, placed her hand on Kyle's mouth, motioning him to stop. Her eyes opened wide as she took a few staccato breaths and reaching down into her handbag pulled out a crushed and wrinkled up piece of paper.

She handed the crumpled paper to Kyle. He carefully unfurled the paper. Stuck together at its corners with faded typing, it was the poem that Kyle gave to Denise before Christmas at Traver's Table 12 years ago.

Kyle whispered in surprise, "You kept this?"

"Of course ... the only poem anyone ever wrote for me. Didn't you want me to keep it?"

Kyle raised his two hands to touch her face, but put them back on his lap, not wanting to alter a moment that was so emotional for him.

Another opportune interruption ensued as the curtains in front of them were drawn open. The two wait staff came forward looking at Kyle as one said, "With your permission?"

Nodding his head, Kyle triggered the next special segment of the evening. The two young men removed the cocktail table, placing it to the front left side of the room. Exquisitely, they wheeled in a low dinner table, draped in white linen, black napkins with 5-candle candelabra.

Denise looked at Kyle and inquired, "Are we dining ... here?"

Kyle now in the total flow of his preparations, "My Denise, this is your night, our night, and we will not share it with anyone else, except our delightful wait staff."

With that, a succession of brilliantly prepared courses came to them in perfect order, hors d'oeuvres, fish course, main course, salad course, cheese plate and a specially prepared geode cake with Denise's likeness, taken from her photo on the top.

Despite the exceptional presentations and courses, Denise and Kyle scarcely touched the food.

Midway through the courses, one of the wait staff looked through the curtain as Kyle lifted his hand. Denise noticing this non-verbal nod and a wink between Kyle and the waiter, asked Kyle, "...and what prey tell are you up to now?"

The curtains in front of them opened slightly and a string quartet stepped in and began to serenade them. Denise put down her fork, dabbed the corners of her mouth with her napkin, leaned in to Kyle and spoke in disbelief, "What is this?"

Kyle feeling every bit the pretentious child, said, "Oh it's Mozart, No. 15 in D minor".

In that instant, their serene setting was filled with loud uncontrollable laughter.

Spontaneously, Denise looked at Kyle and almost declared the words that would capture the moment and their lives, "How could I not love you?"

Kyle's face turned from hilarity to unmitigated sincerity. The time of waiting was over. He must open his heart to the unmistakable truth, "There is only one, and Denise was the ONE."

Kyle made one more gesture to the wait staff as they stepped behind the red cashmere couch where Denise and Kyle were seated and drew back curtains that uncovered glass terrace doors.

Denise and Kyle looked over their inside shoulders and watched as the waiters slid the glass doors back. A cool breeze from the second story outdoor deck area touched their faces as the musicians began to play slow, romantic music.

Kyle whispered, "Denise, you are THE ONE. You have always been THE ONE in my life. Will you join me outside on the terrace and dance with me?"

Hand in hand, they walked around the back of the red couch and out onto the terrace.

The breeze increased as Kyle took Denise in his arms, slowly dancing, their eyes never leaving the other.

The first droplets of rain fell on the deck with them dancing alone on the terrace, melted together in soft embrace and eyes that speak. This singular minute seemed to be without end as it was meant to be. As the rain strengthened so did the passion of their unstated truths.

Denise's arms were wrapped tightly around Kyle's neck and she reached down for the deepest meaning, the richest of feelings she had ever known. Denise wanted new words, a way to communicate the fullness of her heart without saying words ever said to others.

The rain soaked them, reminiscent of a walk so long ago to Traver's Table. Kyle raised his hands to Denise's face, feeling the rain and tears of joy that graced her cheeks. Placing his face to hers, their chins fitting so perfectly, Denise placed her velvet lips to Kyle's with a tenderness that she had only felt once before on a quiet farm road.

Denise's kiss was a whisper, a private language meant only for Kyle.

The whisper of her kiss was speaking to Kyle. The touch of her lips to his said once and forever more, "I love you".

Kyle kept his eyes on Denise, "the girl". Kyle's hands slide down to her soaked hips, holding Denise in place to stop their dancing movements. He brought his right index finger to her lips, then to his own. There was silence. They were still, except for eyes that both overflowed with the shared undeniable truth of their love.

Kyle placed his hand on his chest and then into his soaked tuxedo jacket. From the inside pocket he took out a very wet little grey box. His hands together, cupped the box, and held it out to her. The knot in his throat, and the rapid beat of his heart brought the words of his mother back to him, "There is only one."

The time was now.

"Denise, I love you!"

Kyle extended his cupped hands holding the grey box to Denise.

Denise's mouth fell slightly open, believing that she knew what the box contained.

There were still a few words to say and Kyle was ready, after all these years to say them to Denise as he opened the box.

He pointed to the diamond on the left, "This is me, incomplete, needing you to complete me."

He pointed to the diamond on the right, "This is you, incomplete, needing me to complete you."

Kyle took Denise's right index finger and placed it on

the larger middle diamond, "Together, this is us, complete, becoming all that our hearts, minds and souls can be."

Kyle took the ring from the box, placed it in Denise's hands, "This now belongs to you."

Denise no longer needing words to speak her heart placed her lips to Kyle's.

If there needed to be an answer **Denise's whisper of a kiss**, delivered it.

Appendix

The Whisper of Your Kiss

Lyrics by
Stephen W. Hoag

Verse 1
ALL OF THOSE TIMES YOU PASSED BY ME
I LONGED TO FEEL YOUR LIPS ... CLOSE TO MINE ... A
LOVE SUBLIME ...
THE WHISPER OF YOUR KISS

Verse 2
ALL OF THOSE DREAMS THAT FILLED MY SLEEP
THERE WAS A GLANCING BREEZE ... ON MY FACE ... A
DIVINE EMBRACE
THE WHISPER OF YOUR KISS

~bridge~
   SILENT PROSE, LOVE'S REPOSE
   ONE CARESS, FROM HEAVEN BLESSED
   HEARTS TO STIR..... WHISSSSSPERRRRRRRRRRRR
   PLEASE GIVE ME THIS BLISS
   I LONG FOR YOUR KISS

Verse 3
NOT IN YOUR ARMS I YEARN TO BE ...

JUST TO YOUR LIPS SO PURE ... MY LIFE BLOOD ... A
PASSION FLOOD
THE WHISPER OF YOUR KISS

Verse 4
SILENTLY SEND YOUR WORDS TO ME
PLEASE JUST ONE KISS TO SHARE ... FOREVER SEALED ...
YOUR LOVE REVEALED
THE WHISPER OF YOUR KISS

~bridge~
SILENT PROSE, LOVE'S REPOSE
ONE CARESS, FROM HEAVEN BLESSED
HEARTS TO STIR..... WHISSSSSPERRRRRRRRRRRRR
PLEASE GIVE ME THIS BLISS
I LONG FOR YOUR KISS

RAIN and Singular Love

by Stephen W. Hoag

The manner in which a unique creation is formed is often one of amazement. As a painting of curiously mounted color or never attempted design, *singular love* is a creation that is rich genuine sentiment that touches the spirit in ways that no one can measure it or adequately articulate its depth.

For a handful of singular love creations the gifts of the natural world are entwined. The sunshine of a spring morning ... the purest white of the fallen snow with its unduplicated flakes of lace and lattice ... and the subtle resonance of the sea rushing to shore are components of someone's singular love admixture.

For the singular love of two people, somewhere far away, but forever close there is the partner of "rain". The rapidity of its presence in their lives regardless of day, time or circumstance, speaks to the <u>singularity of their love</u>.

Rain ... bringing to their faces the damp lushness of tempered emotion, that can neither be measured or checked by limits, large or small, its every drop, like their every shared moment cannot be replicated despite their propensity to reprise precipitous moments, while creating even greater exhilaration as their love flourishes in new layers.

In a concert of perceptibly unconnected pieces, there is synergy. Just as each drop of rain is so exquisitely perfect, the drops may combine to form waves of water or sprinklings on rose petals. For those of a singular love momentary whispers or insouciant movements, may together form a fabric of sound that uncloaks the ear from distraction or brings forth the surging somatic power of their desires.

It is the "rain", through no choice of their own, that has bound them in mind, body and spirit. In each manifestation of falling rain, no matter the moment, it serves as a reminder of their singular love, evoking the shared memories and those yet to come.

Acknowledgments

The years of writing "Whisper of a Kiss" is the confluence of a lifetime of observations, influences, and teaching moments, but none more inspirational than the impact of a single individual. The powerful concept of how one person can alter the life path of another is at the essence of "Whisper of a Kiss".

The number of wonderful people who unknowingly touched this piece is endless, but the young men, their mothers, advocates, and my incredible Academic Mentor team of the Developing Tomorrow's Professionals program are most prominent. To that end I acknowledge George Coleman, Stefan Pryor, Paul Flinter, James Granfield, Robert Felder, Jesse K. Davis, Jarom Freeman, Jermaine Brookshire Jr., Jason Bastos Pereira, Andre Armour, Akintunde Sogunro, Gilbert Agyeman, Mario Callahan II, and Silverberg Ayree.

To the scores of schools I have worked with these 40 years past, thank you for allowing me to serve your students and faculty. I would particularly like to express my gratitude to Norristown Area High School, Norristown, Pennsylvania and Lyman Hall High School, Wallingford, Connecticut for providing some of the images reflected in this book.

To family members and close friends, thank you for the many years of support and encouragement that brought about this writing from concept to the fullest manifestation of its intended purpose. Special appreciation is extended to Gina Hoag, Maureen DiSorbo, Kathleen Hoag, Tommy Hoag, Barry O'Brien, John Hrehowsik, George Lehrer, and Alex Lehrer.

Special thanks to the tremendously talented Tony Falcone for creating the silhouette of "Whisper of a Kiss" central character, "The One", Denise.

About the Author

An innovative and passionate educator, Dr. Hoag was a member of the Connecticut State Department of Education for over 35 years. An accomplished speaker, he has entertained and thrilled audiences throughout his lifetime with his anecdotes and philosophy on teaching, parenthood, athletic coaching and leadership. Dr. Hoag has received state and national recognition for teaching, coaching, education assessment and community service. Of note, he was the recipient of the national 2008 C. Thomas Olivio Award, presented to one person annually for leadership and creativity in student assessment by the National Occupational Competency Testing Institute; the 2013 Silver Eagle Award of the Connecticut Council of Deliberation for "sterling service to uplift humanity"; and the 2016 Outstanding Community Service Award by the Urban League of Greater Hartford. Dr. Hoag created and directed the ground breaking Developing Tomorrow's Professionals (DTP) program for Black and Hispanic young men. Stephen Hoag is the author of "A Son's Handbook, Bringing Up Mom with Alzheimer's/Dementia" a stirring personal account of his ten years caring for his mother with this dreaded disease.

Made in the USA
Middletown, DE
10 June 2020